LIVE FAST before your clock strikes **12**

LIVE FAST
before your clock strikes 12

Reb & Dran
HAND-IN HAND

Vivian Ward Newton

PALMETTO
PUBLISHING
Charleston, SC
www.PalmettoPublishing.com

Copyright © 2024 by Vivian Ward Newton

All rights reserved
No portion of this book may be reproduced, stored in a retrieval system, or transmitted in any form by any means—electronic, mechanical, photocopy, recording, or other—except for brief quotations in printed reviews, without prior permission of the author.

First Edition

Hardcover ISBN: 979-8-8229-3823-6
Paperback ISBN: 979-8-8229-3824-3

Table of Contents

Dedication ix
Preface 1
Prologue 9
    The Story of Gua 9
    The Story of the Clock 13
    Similarities of Human and Bear 19
Where Did It All Begin? 24
Reb's Parents and His Mysterious Birth 26
    A Mysterious Birth 30
Dran's Parents and His Mysterious Birth 37
    Dran's Mother 40
    Dran's Parents Meet 41
    Continuing Animal Care 42
    Dran's Birth 45
    From the Thoughts of Dran 49
    Siblings 55
Emphasized Differences Dispelled 57
Life of Reb and Dran: 00:01 a.m. to 06:00 a.m. 63
    Reb and His Innocent Trouble 63
    Dran and Benno 70
    6:00 a.m. Encounter at the Animal Reserve 78
    It's 6:00 a.m. 88
    A Time of Beginning and Growth 89

Life of Reb and Dran: 06:00 a.m. to 12:00 p.m. Noon....91
    Reb Begins to Find His Purpose....................91
    Reb's Friendship with Storm......................102
    Reb's Siblings, His Forever Friends.................109
    Dran's School Friend, Boss 114
    Dran's Siblings, His Eternal Friends and Confidants....124
    Dran's Acceptance Letter.........................129
    Encounter at the Outdoor Theater 136
    It's 12:00 Noon..................................144
    A Time to Bloom and Achieve:....................145
    Attributes at 06:01 to 12:00 p.m. 145

Life of Reb and Dran: 12:00 p.m. Noon to 6:00 p.m.....147
    Reb Against All Odds: The Big Protest..............147
    Dran's Relocation and Exploring New Horizons.......158
    Encounter at the Strawberry Patch 169
    It's Six O'Clock 178
    A Time to Transform and Become:.................179
    Attributes at 12:01 p.m. to 06:00 p.m. 179

Life of Reb and Dran: 6:00 p.m. to 11:59 p.m. 180
    Reb Helping Others.............................180
    Dran Gives Back to Gua 188
    Encounter at the Celebration..................... 200
    It's 11:59 p.m...................................209
    A Time to Reflect and Harvest:...................210
    Attributes at 06:00 p.m. to 11:59 p.m. 210

Life of Reb and Dran at Midnight................... 211
   Reb Unites with Dran........................... 211
   Dran Unites with Reb...........................220
   It's Midnight 232
   A Time of Reward: Attributes at Midnight...........234

Appendix: It Helps to Know 235
   The Significance of the Number Twelve.............235
   Religious and Cultural Significance of Twelve.........236
   The Significance of Life........................... 241
   The Significance of Time..........................246
   The Significance of the Tree 251

Dedication

To my precious son: I saw you roar. I saw you soar You are my Reb and Dran. You were and still are "brave like a bear."

To my dear husband Herbert: I love you for your unwavering patience and always having an encouraging word. Thank you for your willingness to travel the beaches of the world together. It is great sharing our lives.

To our children, H. Bernard, Benita, Doshandra, and Tabatha: you have learned from me, yet you have been some of my greatest teachers. Our bond of love is sustained.

To my precious grandchildren, who have expanded my capacity to love beyond measure.

To my dear siblings: blood relates us, but our years of support and encouragement have made you some of my closest friends.

To my dear friends, who have enhanced my life and helped to create some of my fondest memories.

To my angel friends, whose midnight clock struck without fanfare. You are loved and missed.

To my precious ancestors, who laid a solid foundation in which we all must continue to build.

PREFACE

I WAS BORN IN AN ERA WHEN THERE WERE FREQUENT outbursts of social unrest throughout the United States. There were civil rights demonstrations, strikes, and civil disorders. Political protests were common occurrences throughout the country. There were unfair wages, substandard houses, and many other discrepancies throughout the country. Unfortunately, there are similar occurrences in our modern day.

Being in the rural South was where I experienced one of the greatest breeding grounds and threats for racial violence. There were spoken and unspoken boundaries that kept select people within the invisible walls of segregation.

From childhood to adulthood, there was always a gnawing and agitation within me. The question for me was, why were there limitations placed on the lives of equal citizens within this community?

I would later become aware that this behavior was not unique to our community but prevalent throughout the South. This behavior was not even unique to the United States but one of the stains of injustice throughout the world.

Through these prejudices, I witnessed strong determination. Many would not accept that their life's fate would be determined by an ill-willed person of any ideology or color. The idea of being in control of your own destiny was an incentive enough to explore other options.

My parents were some of the ones that became a part of the Great Migration. There were approximately six million blacks that moved from the American South to northern, midwestern, and western states from 1910 until the 1970s. Their goal was to seek greater employment opportunities beyond the fields of the South. Though it often meant separation from families, it was a worthwhile risk for the potential benefits.

My parents relocated to New Jersey in the early 1950s. There were established relatives living there already, and they assisted in my parents' acclimation to this unfamiliar environment. The adage, "Be the hand that lifts others up," was a recurring theme for many years. I witnessed the doors at my parents' home welcoming others who needed a place to temporarily reside during their adaptation.

There were, however, many positive attributions to life in the rural community of Anson County, North Carolina. The black community was protective and supportive of one another. These close-knit neighborhoods were dependable. The children and adults worked, played, and worshiped together. The elders were respected as well as the community leaders of morticians, preachers, and teachers. There were few distractions. Between school, church, and home, you were engaged in many positive, character-building activities. There was a genuine desire of the elders to assist the younger generation. Their encouragement was for them to prepare for a successful future, defy any stereotypes, and dispel any negative labels. Numerous students were inspired, and levels of achievement took root throughout our area. These feats produced a community of accomplished, skilled, and talented individuals. They were proficient in many disciplines. Despite many odds, determination bred undeniable success.

My childhood life was a fluctuation of a North/South residence between parents and grandparents. Yearly, I along with my siblings made our pilgrimage to the North, and it solidified my belief that there were viable options available in my world. My exposure to life past the Mason–Dixon line opened my eyes to a contrasting environment. I did, however, realize that the North was not a utopia. Some of the same situations experienced in the South were experienced in the North as well. The diversity of people and color variants allowed racism to be experienced more discreetly. Some situations were not done as blatantly, yet with equivalent results to the South.

As we study the history of the United States, we realize we are a country made up of many nationalities and cultures. There are obvious differences, yet none of us are more entitled than the next. The Declaration of Independence states that "All men are created equal." The melting pots of races bring flavors to our country to enhance all our lives. This perspective humbles any exalted view of ourselves. The harmonic nature of all creatures is necessary for ultimate survival. Everything and everyone has a purpose.

There is an abundance of similarities that could not be denied if we relinquish the focus of the smidgen number of differences. There is always something you will find that you have in common with one another. The perspective of changing the outlook could increase the expansion of the mind and a variety of life experiences. There are immediate benefits for all involved.

The behavior of people became such a persistent curiosity in my life that I decided to pursue this study in my college career. My undergraduate college degrees are in psychology and education. Eventually, I obtained an advanced degree in counseling. My ultimate goal was to gain knowledge of the understanding of the mind and then teach for lasting change.

However, if there is change, there must first be a personal desire, and then the mind must be renewed with replacement information. This is the process of learning, and this is the breeding ground for true transformation.

When I attended college in Greensboro, North Carolina, I had already developed a love for writing and had been emphatically encouraged by my high school English teacher to "Never put down your pen." She was moved to tears by a poem I had written in the tenth grade. It was at that time I realized the power of pen and paper to move others when you write from your heart. I accepted that tenth-grade challenge, and I have kept my pen moving. I have found writing to be a stress reliever, a thought clarifier, and a method for self-discovery. It can be a method used for therapeutic healing. Writing directs the creative energy to assist in imagination and achievements.

In 2019, we experienced a life-altering event in our family with the loss of our only son. In all our training and learning, nothing prepared us for the turbulent emotional grief of this loss. That event shook our core.

Writing was the thing that mentally saved me. It was therapeutic to put thoughts on paper freely and without judgment. I could smile, laugh, scream, sulk, or cry all with the stroke of a pen. It also rekindled some of my thoughts from early years.

It was those thoughts from years of wondering what our impact on life could be if we pushed our way through murkiness with boldness and confidence. What if we listened to our hearts instead of allowing others' opinions to take up so much of our head space. What if we accepted encouragement from others that cross our paths and dispel the negativity that seeks to discourage us?

Each situation that is presented could be the catalyst for our accepting any roles we can contribute for change.

Instead of avoidance, it is imperative to consider that there are giants that can fall because we challenge instead of evade.

This era of time we are here is our chronicle of history. It is his story or her story that allows us to stamp the clock and seal the legacy.

When my husband and I began our own family, we strived to expose our children to the vastness of the world. As life would have it, we were a military family, and diversity was a built-in part of military life. Our travel in and out of the country expanded our knowledge of other cultural norms. It paved the way for more empathy and compassion. It took us from our familiar settings and helped us see the world from a unique perspective. We watched our children flourish from the benefits of diversity. They were accepting and inquisitive, which ultimately produced tolerance.

Authoring this book was inspired by the precious life of my son. His example and his legacy was seeking out the absolute best in everybody. He accepted people at face value. He explored the similarities we have among us, and he remained open to learning from his youngest to his oldest encounter. He enjoyed life and explored different avenues hurriedly as if he knew his limited time. He showed us by example that opening your heart and mind brings self-awareness, and it can come from unlikely sources. You do not have to look hard or far to find it. It can be all around you.

LIVE FAST before your clock strikes 12

In reflection of our son's life, I pondered his personality and his contributions to our family and to society. It was particularly meaningful to acknowledge the significance of limited time.

Not only do we acknowledge our willingness to give of ourselves and share our lives, but we must also acknowledge that our contributions are contingent on the days that we are given to occupy this earth.

12:00 a.m. to 12:00 midnight consists of twenty-four hours. This cycle completes an entire day. Many things can be accomplished or other things undone based on our minute-by-minute decisions.

The constant movement of the clock correlates to the constant movement of time in our lives.

What will we do with the limited time we have in this world?

Will we live with purpose and with intention?

Will we develop an urgency to prioritize purpose?

Will you give your decision-making power over to someone else?

Will you acknowledge that our clocks begin the minute we are born?

Will we acknowledge that each one of our personal clocks will strike twelve midnight, and our day is done?

In this book, our two main characters, Reb and Dran, similarly take us on the journey of awareness and adventure. The intertwining in their lives causes us to wonder who or what among us is assisting in our life's journey. Neither of them could not imagine the role each would play in the other's life.

PROLOGUE
The Story of Gua

GUA IS A WELL-PRESERVED CITY THAT BOASTS OF MANY breathtaking geographical features.

These characteristics of Gua would be ones to include in any beautiful painting.

It has a sheer natural landscape, yet the appearance is magical and mystical.

Due to the variance in seasons, occasionally it flaunts the icy mountains as well as the warm coastal landscapes. The other picturesque scene is the dense forest and wooded terrains.

The mountains provide the perfect panoramic view around the city.

The overall view in Gua is a marvel to behold.

The temperature is an ideal ambient average range of 64 to 75 degrees.

The configuration of living space is aesthetically pleasing.

It is a place of beautiful museums and galleries that display the richness of Gua's culture.

There are vast collections of art, including works by local and world-renowned artists.

There are dining options where traditional as well as exotic foods are available. Some restaurants sit on the desirable waterfronts.

The aromas in the city are the ones created by nature. There are the smells of rain. There are the smells from the terra-cotta buildings baked by the sun. Of course, the sweet-smelling plants and trees throughout the city and countryside dominate much of the terrain.

Across the city is detailed ancient architecture. There are inviting public parks and green spaces around the city. Gua is noted for its pristine landscape.

The population is a diverse community where services needed for daily life are within everyone's reach. People live and work in harmony. They thrive for the betterment of all.

There is safety and respect for all people and property. The quality of the community is a desirable cultural hub. Education and worship are accessible for all.

The long sun fills the days, and the gorgeous starlit nights offer delightful openings and closings of the day.

It is understandable why so many people seek to spend some of their time in Gua.

People repeatedly heard that it was well worth the investment of their time.

It was never disappointing. The time spent there was often described as an unforgettable experience. There was usually the desire to repeat the experience as soon as possible.

Gua is not utopian, but it is striving to reach that goal. The attempt to duplicate the uniqueness of Gua has failed in many parts of the country. Many have come close but have not perfected the antiquated details.

The infrastructure is well-developed. They are the basis for the economy and quality of life of Gua. There is hard infrastructure like bridges, tunnels, railways, ports, and harbors. These tangible structures are necessary for economic growth, connectivity, and smooth functioning of Gua society. Businesses are attracted to Gua because of this tangible, sophisticated system.

There is an excellent soft infrastructure as well. This system shapes economic and social interactions. This includes institutions and legal, economic, and social systems. There is an excellent transportation system, a communication network, sewage systems, water systems, healthcare, a school system, and a financial system.

This infrastructure determines the rules, norms, and regulations that guide economic activity, foster innovation, and create an environment where businesses can thrive.

The two systems combine for a harmonious whole to maintain a healthy economy.

People are by far the greatest asset to Gua. With all its natural scenic views, the full beauty of Gua is climaxed with the residents. All the beauty that lies within the city limits is great to look at, but the true beauty lies in the lives of the people. The pride that they have in their beloved city caused them to make every effort to keep the city looking beautiful.

The people are overall happy and appreciative. They feel an intense sense of belonging and support from one another. There is a great emotional connection to each generation. They learn from one another. The comfort of living in this atmosphere improves the well-being and motivation of the Gua population. They feel safe there.

It has pedestrian-friendly streets that connect plazas and parks, so that many visitors can explore the city on foot. Several landmarks are within easy walking distance of each other.

There are homes that are situated near businesses. In addition, many workplaces are close by. Schools in nearby neighborhoods are practical. Convenient stores make it easy to access commodities. The streets accommodate cyclists, pedestrians, and public transportation. There are barriers set up to protect pedestrians.

The overall summary of life in Gua is that in all its glory, it is constantly changing to reshape and satisfy the demands of the residents. There is variety and order, which makes any visitor or resident feel that someone is in charge. The streets are full of obvious life. It is full of mystery and obvious attributes. There are great personal gains to dwell in such a beautiful city as Gua. It has many traits that are beautifully described as outside benefits.

The true beauty and happiness within a person are not limited to location. It is possible to create your own Gua in your life. It starts and ends with defining, developing, and maintaining the beauty within yourself. The journey of Reb and Dran brought them to a place of understanding this truth. Wherever life takes you, there are repeated opportunities to discover the beauty in and around us.

The Story of the Clock

The tranquility in Gua was extremely desirable among the constant flow of tourists. You could often witness car license plates from all fifty states. They were all seeking the most talked-about destination of the year. They yearned to seek the experiences in this beautiful atmosphere.

There were quaint shops with unique items that could only be found in Gua. It brought a sense of nostalgia and charm all over the city. Many of these family-owned shops have seen management from several generations.

There was a cobblestone side alley with some of the most unique shopping in the area. There was an old-fashioned drugstore that only sold natural medicines. These medicinal remedies were always the first choice if anyone was experiencing discomfort. Inside the drugstore was an ice-cream counter featuring local churned ice cream. You could see vintage and retro signs lining the walls in the store. They were on display, yet many of them were for sale. There was a tea shop with teas that were locally grown in the residents' gardens.

One of the most interesting shops was one where animals of Gua were created in metal by some local craft metalsmiths. You could not only purchase them, but you could also watch the metalsmiths create their art. There were many other shops that appealed to shoppers searching for unique items.

The most popular attraction in downtown Gua was the street clock. It was one of the most iconic features in the area. The clock was a descendent of an Egyptian Revival clock. It had been donated by a local family who had vacationed in Egypt. They felt it was one of the most magnificent clocks they had ever seen as they browsed in the antique shops. This masterpiece caught their eye, but there were a couple of major concerns. They had to get it back home, and they could not display it in their home. They were so impressed with the beauty of it that they had to figure out a way. They concluded that one of the more practical solutions was to purchase the clock as a gift for the city of Gua and have it shipped across the massive waters back home. If they bought it for the city, they could still see it every day. They carried out the plan by

LIVE FAST before your clock strikes 12

purchasing the magnificent clock and made the necessary arrangement for transport.

When they returned to Gua, they began to share that the city would be receiving a huge surprise. Rumors began to spread as to what it could be. The residents only knew it was coming from Egypt. It took weeks to arrive, but there were people lined up in the streets to witness the big reveal.

With a huge round of applause, the people were ecstatic to see this magnificent piece.

They were extremely grateful for the citywide gift from their fellow residents.

The clock was made of marble and red onyx. The face of the clock was an antique green with gold hands enclosed in glass. There was a shimmer on the clock's face that caused a sparkle when the night fell. It illuminated the streets. It served as a citywide nightlight. It was about twelve feet tall and six feet wide.

The location of the clock in the city was perfect for people to see it every day in their travels.

You could hear the soothing ticks as you walked past it.

It was often said that the clock was the perfect meeting place to get all the firsthand gossip.

The clock had been functioning as a traditional timepiece for many decades. It had become an icon downtown. All these generations later, the clock still stood in its original position on the corner of Broad Street and Forest Road.

The beauty of the clock was a backdrop for many photo opportunities. Families would gather there to commemorate milestone celebrations and holidays. Most households had pictures of their family members standing by the clock.

The clock would strike with a big *bong* sound daily at 6:00 a.m., twelve noon, 6:00 p.m., and twelve midnight. It had been designed to correlate with the movement of the town citizens. The day started for many residents at 6:00 a.m., lunch was at twelve noon, most businesses closed at 6:00 p.m., and twelve midnight was bedtime.

The residents of the town had once complained about the loud *bong* at 12:00 a.m., since it could disturb some people's sleep. It took so long for the case to be heard by the city council that the residents eventually dropped the complaint and accepted the noise from the clock. It was all a part of the uniqueness of Gua.

In February of 1978, there had been a blackout in town. Every business and every home lost electricity, and the city turned completely dark. This was not the first time the city had a blackout. It was usually a quick fix. This was a similar occurrence. The lights were restored in twelve minutes, but this time, a few things had changed. The next time the clock was scheduled to give out the historic *bong*, it failed. Instead, it gave a totally different sound. It was the sound that sounded surprisingly like a growling grizzly bear cub. It was distinct yet somewhat of a soft tone. This was totally unexplainable. The clock did not run on electricity or batteries, so the power outage should have had no effect on the function.

At the next scheduled time at 12:00 a.m., there was no sound at all. The entire clock turned dark for one minute and started ticking again at 12:01 a.m. There was no explanation for such a strange phenomenon. It was incomprehensible.

Stories began to circulate about the history of the clock. There was a mystery about where the clock came from. It was even suggested that someone sabotaged the clock in the twelve-minute blackout. Stories covered the range from *A–Z* with no reputable conclusion.

From that day on, the clock did not strike midnight any longer. Instead, it would strike at 6:00 a.m., 12:00 p.m., and 6:00 p.m. It would darken at twelve midnight with no sound and start again at 12:01 a.m.

Engineers and technicians were summoned to come to Gua to try their hands at fixing the clock, but there were no successes. The clock still refused to strike at 12:00 a.m.

Even though the residents had complained about the noise before, now they really missed the midnight *bong*.

It took a citywide referendum to decide on keeping the clock or replacing this historic piece with a new modern clock and an accurate timepiece. Many began to feel it had served its time and needed to be replaced.

The residents came out in large numbers to vote. There were only a few people interested in replacing the clock, but by the time the votes were cast, they had even changed their minds.

It was such a part of Gua that no one wanted to see it go.

With a resounding majority, the citizens decided to keep the clock with an explanation encrypted on a plaque posted on the ground next to it. With a sense of humor, they wrote:

I want to strike at midnight.
I want to hear my *bong*.
But I am at a loss for words,
for the cat has got my tongue.

They did not want to give up the beauty the clock brought to the landscape in downtown Gua.

They were so elated about the vote that the city created a tour for each Friday night for a "Clock Watch." They hoped that they would be the ones to see the clock resume its duties. It had now become an even larger attraction for all the people living there as well as the many tourists. It became known as the clock avoiding midnight.

LIVE FAST before your clock strikes 12

Similarities of Human and Bear

To change the trajectory of life requires a perspective that will intensify your ability to see.

It requires penetration beyond the natural eyes as you view from the depths of your heart.

When we examine the things we have in common, we often recognize a portion of ourselves in others. We begin to see how each life can intertwine and mutual benefits become inevitable.

Here, you will examine the lives of two distinct beings. They are improbable comparisons which seemingly have nothing in common between the two of them.

The life of a grizzly bear and the life of a human boy requires a figment of imagination for any possible analogy. You will see how they share many parallels as they maneuver the various stages of their lives.

Let us look at some of the commonalities.

In the world, the bear is a massive, iconic animal. Throughout history, there have been many stories of terrifying encounters with humans. Many of these encounters have been exaggerated. The suggested encounters have often been attributed to fear of the strength of the bear. Bears do not typically attack a human unless they are threatened or provoked, much as a human does. They are cautious of one another.

The bear's age is two years for each human year.

According to Wikipedia, the human is the most common and widespread species of primate.

There is a current world population of approximately eight billion people. Though humans vary in many traits (such as genetic predispositions and physical features), any two humans are at least 99 percent genetically similar. It is believed that we and grizzly bears have somewhere between 80 and 90 percent of our genes in common (http://www.humananimalsblog.wordpress.com).

The bear and human are both omnivores.

They hunt and eat salmon, and so do humans.

A den is like a bears' home.

They can stand on their two hind legs as humans.

Humans and bears have evolved.

Bears lose teeth at an early age, and so do humans.

X and Y chromosomes. Males are larger than females, which is true in humans, biologically speaking.

Bears are solitary creatures, although they may come together as a large source of food, and this means that they create a social hierarchy based on their ages and sizes. Humans also create social hierarchy, and possibly because of the same reasons.

Female bears will hum or bleat when they are communicating with their cubs, much like a human communicates with sound.

Female bears have been known to adopt stray cubs, and humans also adopt.

LIVE FAST before your clock strikes 12

Bears fish, and so do humans.

Bears are featured in literature such as "Goldilocks and the Three Bears," and so are humans.

Bears survived the last ice age, and so did humans.

Bears can open jars and unlock door latches, and humans can also do this.

Bears can run at speeds of 25 to 30 mph, and the running speed of humans is said to be 27.44 mph.

Bears have been found to be particularly good at visual tasks involving color, much like humans can.

Bears can learn and very quickly understand the differences between shapes, much like humans can.

Bears can climb; so can humans.

Bears can swim; so can humans.

Bears can be active at any time of day or night, and so can humans.

Bears are territorial of their homes or land, and so are humans.

Bears dig out their own dens, and some humans build their own houses.

Bears can feed anytime; so can humans.

Bears can be clumsy; so can humans.

Bears can be adventurous; so can humans.

Giant pandas have thumbs, and so do humans.

Giant pandas communicate with each other with sounds, and so do humans.

Giant pandas do not hibernate, and neither do humans.

Giant pandas can digest cellulose, which is an important part of green plants and their cell walls. Humans can also digest cellulose.

Giant pandas produce milk to feed their cubs, and so do humans.

Polar bears court each other, and so do some humans.

Some humans like to mate in privacy, and so do polar bears.

Polar bear cubs like to play, and so do human babies.

Polar bear mothers discipline their cubs when they misbehave, and so do some human parents with their children.

Polar bears tend to use their right forelimb more often than their left. Humans have been found to also choose one hand to perform certain tasks more frequently than the other.

Polar bears wash in water; so do humans.

Polar bears have been known to cuddle when sleeping; so do humans.

Humans have families, and so do polar bears.

Sloth bears have lips, and so do humans.

Hair can grow in the ears of a sloth bear, and this can be the same for humans.

Sloth bears' back legs are knee-jointed, and so are humans'.

Sloth bears can bark, grunt, snarl, woof, yelp, shriek, whimper, huff, gurgle, hum, and croon. Humans can make all these noises.

LIVE FAST *before your clock strikes* **12**

As you see, the comparisons support the idea that we share kindred traits, and it is imperative that we find ways to coexist.

Bears settle in places like the ones humans like. They dwell in reliable areas that will supply the necessary resources for survival. The natural richness of the area influences humans and bears in remarkably similar ways.

Bears are not companions of men, but children of God, and His charity is broad enough for both. We seek to establish a narrow line between ourselves and the feathery zeros we dare to call angels but ask a partition barrier of infinite width to show the rest of creation its proper place. Yet bears are made of the same dust, as we breathe the same winds and drink the same waters. A bear's days are warmed by the same sun, his dwellings are over-domed by the same blue sky, and his life turns and ebbs with heart-pulsing like ours and was poured from the same fountain...

—**John Muir**

VIVIAN WARD NEWTON

Where Did It All Begin?

In life, there are mysteries
our eyes cannot behold.
There are stories happening all around
that gradually unfold.
The sun rises for another day.
The seconds pass without delay.
You cannot redo yesterday.
It is time the history books will behold.

LIVE FAST before your clock strikes 12

The story of Reb and Dran
expands decades of time.
It takes them across to many lands.
Showing obstacles, they would climb.
Reb, the curious grizzly bear,
and Dran, the inquisitive man,
realized they had lots to share.
Let us see how it all began.
What did they do to make it through?
We will see it all revealed.
A bond that joined them all their days
helped them both to heal.
Tick, tick, tick, tock—they have begun their race.
There is no time to linger; they must keep up their pace.
Tick, tick, tick, tock—time is moving. There is no time to review.
They will run with gust and vigor until the race is through.
Tick, tick, tick, tock—be aware of the
signs of the strikes from the clock.

REB'S PARENTS
and His Mysterious Birth

GRIZZLY BEARS ORIGINATED IN ASIA AROUND 1.3 MILlion years ago. They evolved from Etruscan bears that appeared in Europe about 5 million years before. Brown bears (*Ursus arctus*) crossed the Bering land bridge some 200,000 years ago. These bears eventually developed into grizzly bears.

This was bear history that Dran's parents had learned and would proudly continue to share.

They had also traced their lineage through several generations. They were extremely proud and grateful for the sacrifices and strength their ancestors had demonstrated and endured.

Both of Reb's sets of great-grandbearparents were the first generation in Gua. They had traveled with a large, migrated group. It had taken many months of travel to reach the area, but they trusted that it would be worth it. They had decided to make the journey because of the circulating rumor of the beautiful habitat with bountiful food, rivers and streams, and lush woodlands and forests. It sounded too ideal to pass up.

Once they settled in this unique environment, they enjoyed all its beauty and the amenities Gua provided for them. They all considered it one of the best decisions they had ever made.

Reb's parents had never known the harshness of other areas their ancestors endured. Though they would often hear stories from the older generation, it sounded like it was a struggle to persevere. Some of the conditions sounded extremely grueling, but it spoke to their strength and determination to survive.

It became motivation for the current generation to strive and reach the standard that they had exemplified.

The third generation had lived in Gua in relative peace and harmony, yet they had begun to see some subtle changes take place.

They could still mingle freely, but with more caution. They still had opportunities to experience a social life with other bears their age. The home range was the gathering place for fun times.

Reb's parents had seen one another at the range and various areas throughout the forest from time to time. They had caught each other's eye but never pursued a lasting conversation.

Generally, the yearling bear would not mingle with the opposite gender during their playful times.

The month of May had arrived, which is the beginning of a typical mating season.

Reb's father had a genuine interest in his mom, but he knew that things did not come that easy. He had to compete for her attention. Reb's mom was also smitten and was hoping that they would soon begin to date.

Both of their wishes came true, and they soon began a ritualized courtship. It included activities like chasing and wrestling as playful interaction.

This relationship quickly progressed from friendship to courtship.

The most serious leap of all came with the decision to start a family.

This mating season would be the one when this special bear cub was conceived.

With total excitement, they began the parenthood journey. Time moved rather quickly, and before you knew it, birth was imminent.

Mom Sow had waited about two hundred days (about six and a half months) from the time of impregnation. Mom Sow began gorging herself on whatever food she could find. During the summer months, that food often consisted of berries and vegetables. She would add fresh salmon as a wonderful way to store fat and gain the weight needed. She strived to store as much fat as possible so that she would have stored fat for survival during the winter months when she would not eat.

LIVE FAST *before your clock strikes* 12

Mom began looking around to find a site suitable for a birthing den. She knew it might take quite a while to find it, so she started in the summer months. She evaluated various locations. She considered a hollow tree and a log. She looked in a cave to see if it would meet her needs. The decision was harder than she initially thought it would be. She took her time, because she wanted the very best for her new baby cub. She finally decided that the cave was her best option for her den.

She prepared the birthplace with extra bedding, with leaves and pine needles to make the space more comfortable for herself and the cub.

As she got closer to delivering her cub, she entered a state of stupor, which was like a light hibernation. Mom Sow's body temperature, breathing, and heart rate all decreased. At this stage, her baby cub began growing again to prepare for the early winter delivery.

A Mysterious Birth

Within the confines of this beautiful city, an unusual occurrence took place. It was an unexplainably sweltering February day. It had been freezing weather prior to that day, but overnight, there was a heat wave that settled over the forest. It was puzzling, because some of the animals still witnessed snow outside the forest's barriers.

The heat was only in the confines of the forest area, and the sun beamed a bright light right in the center of it all. It was a strange phenomenon that threw the animals' rhythm off and into a troubling frenzy. They tried not to panic, but it took all the effort they could muster. They attempted to go about their daily lives, but it was extremely uncomfortable with the beaming sun. With the drastic weather change, they had an eerie feeling that something major was about to happen.

This time of year was considered the birthing season for the bear cubs. There was nervous excitement throughout the forest, as many sow bears were preparing for their upcoming births.

The birthing season was a predictable time for the bear community. It had been a time of anticipation and preparation since the summer months. Now the time had finally arrived.

Most of the unborn cubs' development had taken place mainly in the last two months. This was due to the developmental process called delayed implantation.

LIVE FAST before your clock strikes 12

There had been some births in January, which is a typical time for cub births. There were only a few mom sows that were still anxiously awaiting the opportunity to welcome their cubs.

One of the sow bears had prepared for her first cub's arrival for months. Her mating had taken place during the summer. The time had now arrived for the debut of her little cub. She had prepared the den with extra bedding to serve as a buffer between them and the cold ground.

Her body was well prepared with all the excessive eating she had done to become obese. She needed to store fat to support her and her cub until spring. She knew she would lose much of the weight during her time of hibernation. She had become a masterful forager during the preparation time.

Before his birth, the bear cub had been comfortable in the cocoon of his mother's body. He stayed nice and warm and was well-fed daily with his mother's nutrients. He had been in the dark and wet bed of her womb for about six months, but during that time, he had grown. He was small enough to still move around with little effort. He would just eat, sleep, and grow. Somehow though, he knew this was not a permanent residence. It would be just a matter of time.

On the twelfth day in February, it happened. His world as he knew it changed forever. Suddenly, there was lots of motion going on. He felt his mother's body jerking and moving sporadically. Reb had no idea what was happening to himself or to his mother.

He began to slide down a long, slippery tunnel. Without any effort of his own, he entered a narrow and curvy path. He was not so sure he wanted to go, but he did not have a choice. Because bear cubs cannot see for many days after birth, he was not aware that the darkness was quickly becoming light. All that he could do was go along with whatever was happening to him. He was excited and afraid simultaneously. In his heart, he felt that he was going someplace that would be dramatic and transformative. He could not help but think of the question, "Where will this lead me, and what will I find when I get there?"

Little did he know how much his physical existence was about to change. A new reality was awaiting, and it was exploding with a capital *E*!

Whoosh! Just like riding on a sliding board, fast and furious, the tiny bear cub slid completely out from his mother's body.

In a dark cave nestled in a beautiful, thick, and enchanted forest, the tiny bear cub was born. The day of his birth had been strange with the unexplainable heatwave. It was only in the area that the new cub was born. The entire animal community was still confused as to how this could happen, especially in the month of February.

There were other strange things about that day. This bear cub was the only one born within those twenty-four hours. This was particularly unusual since there were still mom sows waiting for their delivery. He was also a single birth, whereas many sows had up to five cubs in their litter at the time of delivery.

LIVE FAST before your clock strikes 12

The cub was nine inches long and weighed a mere 1.2 pounds. You would think a larger cub would come from such a large mom sow. He would learn later that this was an average size for most bear cubs at birth. He had fine hair that caused him to look hairless. He was tiny, but based on his mother and father's size, they were confident that in just a matter of time, he would be the big grizzly bear he was meant to be.

Things felt different for the bear cub. He was not sure if that was good or bad, but he felt free. Now there were even more questions. Who? What? When? Where? And how? They bombarded his mind and were coming rapid-fire. He had no answers available to him, so he quickly concluded that he would have to allow things to continue to unfold. He did not know how long his freedom would last before he had to travel through that tunnel again. He felt an urgency to make the most of the time he had and to do it as quickly as possible.

Surprisingly, the sun ceased its bright shine, and the clouds filled the sky again. Within minutes, the snow began to fall, and the weather was back at its seasonal cold temperature. There had been an immediate drop of over 80 degrees. There had never been a marvel recorded in the history of Gua like this.

After the brief weather shift, things were back to normal. They were experiencing the freezing weather that was expected this time of year.

The little bear cub was cold and shaking. His mom quickly grabbed him and held him tight. This compassionate act from his mother brought him immediate comfort. He felt safe knowing he was in secure arms.

Mom Sow licked her formless cub clean and began to mold his shapeless body to resemble a bear. Her process of nurturing had begun. It required much patience to prepare him to survive in the challenging world outside the den. Mom Sow's goal was to get him to five pounds before his emergence from the cave in the spring.

Reb's birth continued to be a major topic of discussion. The circumstances surrounding his birth seemed scary to the other animals. The bear community talked among themselves about the unusual weather. It was calm all around the forest. The forest was awkwardly silent for miles around. The only sound that was heard was the city clock that bellowed a big *bong*. Other than that, it was as if all the animals were all asleep. Instead, all their eyes were glued toward the cave. Something exciting was happening. They would all wait for the emergence of the special bear cub. There had to be something incredibly special about this new bear cub. Days passed, and they saw no movement, yet they continued their watch.

When the day finally came, the animals saw Mom Sow come to the door of the cave. Suddenly, all the animals began to move closer. They all wanted to be the first to see the mystifying cub.

LIVE FAST *before your clock strikes* 12

Finally, they saw the little paws close under Mom Sow. The animals erupted to loud roars as a cheer. They had seen what they all had been waiting for.

Later that day, the announcement was made that the new bear cub had a name. His name was Reb. That was a strange name to the animal community. Why was he given that name? Would that mean he resists or opposes the order of establishment? Would he defy the rules? Would he be a rebel?

No one had the answers now, but they all believed Reb was destined to do remarkable things.

When Reb arrived, Mom had done everything in preparation. She was not in any way disappointed. Reb was all she expected him to be and more. He was the most handsome cub her eyes had ever seen. She had no apprehension but was fully committed to loving and protecting her little cub.

For the next seven weeks (about one and a half months), they remained in the den. Mom Sow invested her full attention in all his needs. She had not eaten or drunk anything for several months but was now desperate for a drink.

Reb's parents were excited and surprised to have his single birth. They were in total agreement with the bear community that they believed he was a special cub.

The parents even did things different from the traditional cub-rearing. Father boar bears usually have nothing to do with the cub once he is born. Normally, Mom Sow handled all the responsibilities. Rebs' father was involved more than traditionally done. He had prepared with Reb's mom to welcome him.

Mom sow was extremely attentive to Reb. She fed him from her stored fat for about 6 months. She protected him from predators because of his vulnerability from cougars, wolves and even to other bears.

Mom Sow then resumed her foraging to bring in the necessary nutrients to keep Reb healthy and well. She taught Reb some survival skills and made it known that now that he would become an opportunistic feeder, eating what was available. That would be until he perfected his hunting skills.

Reb's birth had been utterly unique, but so was the little cub, Reb.

All the training was necessary, because Reb would soon have a baby sister cub in the fall of the second year. Mom Sow was then extremely busy taking care of two cubs, but she figured out the things she needed to do to make it all work. It was very gratifying for Mom Sow to see the interaction of the siblings. Reb even helped his mom out sometimes with his sister.

Mom shared her time with them both and found time to give them the individual undivided attention they both desired.

DRAN'S PARENTS
and His Mysterious Birth

DRAN'S PARENTS HAD MADE SURPRISING DISCOVERIES about the genealogy of their ancestors. It had always been a passionate area of interest for them both, so they delved into any available resources they could find to expand their knowledge. They were particularly interested in how both families migrated to the city of Gua generations ago.

Their knowledge of their family history traced them to the continent of Africa. Dran's family were descendants of enslaved people brought from the homelands of Africa by force to work in the New World. Their rights were nonexistent. There was physical suffering at the hands of the slave owners. Families were separated, and many lives were lost.

It took many years of suffering and different movements or demonstrations to gain any momentum for lasting change.

It even consisted of a Civil War to bring any resolution of slavery. The Emancipation Proclamation in 1863 was a crucial document in granting the new reality.

Dran's great-great-grandparents had been a part of slavery. His great-grandparents were the first-generation voters in political elections in the United States. Dran's grandparents had been a part of the Great Migration in the twentieth century, and his parents were a part of the Civil Rights movement. There had been generations of political involvement.

Each decade brought about changes to their present conditions. With the history of the family struggle, Dran's parents knew there was still more to be done. With the decision to have their own family, it was imperative to be an active part of change.

When Dran's parents reflected on the sacrifices of their ancestors, it brought such a sense of pride for the many efforts. The act of the ancestors was to make the world better for the generations to come. Dran's parents were products of a strong group of people, and they would give their families the same commitment they had received.

As they investigated more of how they got to Gua, they found some interesting documents that explained much of it in detail.

These documents revealed that Dran's great-grandparents had been a part of the slave diaspora. His paternal ancestor had worked on a farm under the supervision of a slave master. While he worked diligently, he learned some vital skills, and he became masterful in handling the farm animals. He encompassed many duties on the farm, but his passion was tending the animals. There was an undeniable connection.

The animals were in sync with his commands and offered no resistance to their duties. Instead, they would run to him each morning as a daily greeting.

Within the farm ecosystem, the animals would eat hay and corn grown on the farm. They in turn provided milk, eggs, wool, and meat for humans, and their waste fertilized the soil. They pulled plows and carts. It was a highly organized system created by Dran's great-grandfather to keep things moving efficiently. He provided food and shelter for them and ensured their health and safety. He managed their population to maximize productivity. It was hard to imagine anyone else managing such a proficient farmland.

The slave master and his family had traveled to Gua on a couple of vacations. It had only taken one time to fall in love with the beauty of the city.

He began to think about how their lives could be so different if they could make Gua their permanent home. Once he shared his ideas with his family, they were immediately on board for the change.

Relocation was not the only change. He proposed to his family that they offer the opportunity for Dran's great-grandfather, along with his family, to join them in Gua. They would not go as slaves but as free people, starting a new life in an accepting, beautiful environment. He even offered the finances for them to start their new lives there.

With joy and gratitude, Dran's family accepted the proposal. This began the first generation of free Gua residents for their family.

Things thrived there for everyone. Dran's great-grandfather used the skills he had developed on the farm to provide a lucrative life there. He soon became known as an animal empath. With such an elevated level of sensitivity to other creatures, it was an appropriate title. He could recognize the feelings the animals were experiencing. That interpretation could be if they needed something, whether it was food, love, or even to be left alone. It was a natural gift that he was so drawn to animals.

Over the next decades, this emerging gift became an identifiable trait in the family line.

Dran's Mother

Dran's mother did not have as many details on the ancestry from her family. She was aware that both her paternal and maternal roots derived from Equatorial Guinea near the area of Malabo on Binko. They were a part of the Bubi people indigenous to Bioko. It was once the majority group in the region, but because of war and disease during the Portuguese expedition, it became the number two group.

LIVE FAST before your clock strikes 12

Through the slave trade, Equatorial Guinea was one out of the fifty-plus ethnic groups in African ancestors where most African descendants in America originated.

She was convinced that her family was a part of these groups. She was also aware that they had settled along the East Coast of the United States.

As far as she could tell, her family had been in Gua for three generations. She did not know all the details, but she was glad the decision was made to come to such a beautiful place. Their families had a great life there. She felt that through all her ancestors' suffering, they were minutely compensated by having the privilege of living within the beauty of Gua.

Dran's Parents Meet

Dran's parents attended the same school and met during middle school years. They shared several classes together and quickly became friends.

Their friendship continued for the next six years. Once they graduated from high school, they did not see one another for two years. During that time, they thought of one another very often, but neither made any effort to reach out.

As fate would have it, they saw one another at a reunion, and it was there that they realized they both wanted to pursue a committed relationship. They began to seriously date while they continued to pursue their personal professional goals.

Within two additional years, the first stage of their professional education was complete. They married and made their home in Gua. It was a misnomer to consider living anyplace else.

Dran's parents had waited a few years after marriage to start a family. They wanted to make sure that their lives were in order before any children arrived. Their plan worked as they had scheduled, and soon, they were preparing for their first bundle of joy, Dran. They were overjoyed, and as typical parents, they had great plans for their lives together as a family.

Continuing Animal Care

Many generations later, many family members continued in the field of animal care.

From the time of his birth, Dran's father was constantly surrounded by many four-legged friends.

When he arrived at the restaurant, he shared with lots of excitement what he saw. His friends did not share any of the excitement and were nonchalant about it. They only surmised it as a common sight, especially for such. Neighbors would often seek their family for advice for care for their pets. Their animal knowledge and commitment were irrefutable.

It was predictable that Dran's father would become a professional veterinarian. Animals had become his passion as well. He felt most comfortable in the presence of animals each day. He considered it a privilege to interact and care for animals daily.

LIVE FAST before your clock strikes 12

He soon started his own practice there in Gua, and the residents there were thrilled for the continuing legacy.

One day after a busy day at work, Dran's father stopped to meet some friends for dinner in downtown Gua.

There had been a slight mist of rain before he left work, but as he got closer to the restaurant, there was a sudden downpour. As he passed the historic clock on the corner, a large bolt of lightning struck overhead.

Immediately after the strike, he refocused his eyes on driving. Across the top of the clock, in the clouds, he could clearly see an image of a huge bear floating across the sky. It covered a gigantic portion of his viewpoint. It was not just an object in the sky; it was most of the sky. He did not get a picture, but he could not wait to share what he had just seen.

h an animal lover. They had all seen different objects in cloud formations, but he knew that this was different. He changed the subject as they continued to enjoy the dinner.

Dran's mother was a little more excited when he got home and told the story to her. She wondered, though, if it was just fatigue. She was aware of how hard he worked. She helped him at his office two days per week as she pursued other areas of interest.

Dran's father did not fret. He determined that you had to be there to appreciate the realness of the image.

They got a good night's sleep, but the very next day, they received a call in the office of an injured bear. He typically did not handle many bears, but he agreed to meet the animal control team in the area only a few miles away. They met at the entrance to the forest. It was a delicate and risky endeavor. The other bears in the forest could easily misinterpret their assistance for harm.

As they approached, Dran's father made eye contact with the bear as he lay there in obvious pain. He estimated the bear to be a young teenage yearling but still big enough to be a threat. As they gazed at one another, the bear uttered a small whimper, but did not move. Dran's father assessed that he had an injured leg with a tree branch pierced through.

The animal control team suggested euthanizing the bear to stop the suffering. They would have to call backup to get the proper equipment to move the bear to a facility.

Dran's father had a different suggestion. If they could tranquilize the bear there in the forest, he would do the necessary procedure to remove the tree branch. With reluctance, an agreement was finalized, and the process began. Dran's father completed the procedure, and they all left the forest feeling tired but relieved. They all shared a deep sense of accomplishment.

Dran's father could not forget the needful look in the bear's eyes.

He could not help but think of the bear he had seen in the clouds the day before. Could it all be related? He did not have an answer, but he felt that somehow, it would soon make sense.

Dran's Birth

There was a great deal of activity happening at the health care facility in Gua. It had a reputation of being one of the premier centers in the country. It sat on the edge of the city with a stunning backdrop of towering mountains.

There was an outside garden area where patients and staff often gathered for lunch or times of meditation. Despite it being an active medical center, the garden was a peaceful place.

On this day, February 12, the entire center was very serene. It was a beautiful day with seasonal weather for this time of year. There was light snow, but traveling had not been tedious. The medical center's day had been one of routine care. They were grateful that nothing traumatic had happened.

There was a residential area nearby that was not as peaceful. It was experiencing commotion from a couple preparing to make the trip to the medical center for their child's birth. They had prepared diligently for this day, but instead, it was a little chaotic.

The preparation had been ongoing for many months. They had recently assembled the baby crib and set up the nursery, complete with a welcome sign. This had finalized the tangible preparations. It was such a beautiful room and extremely functional. Now, all that was left was the physical act of delivery and the emotional journey of parenting, which was their greatest concern.

They were a little anxious about the new role they were about to embark on. They were aware that their lives without children would drastically change. Yet, their hope and prayers were that they would be instrumental in the development of this precious bundle of joy. A sincere commitment had been made to learn and grow with their child.

Mom reminded Dad that the time had come to head to the center. She prided herself on the ability to tolerate pain, but the contractions had intensified tremendously. She wanted to get there as soon as she could so they would be in place for this awaited event.

Dad grabbed the packed bag, ran to the car, and placed it in the trunk. His feet made a quick U-turn as he ran back in to help Mom to the car. He assisted her with extreme caution as they trudged through the snow to their waiting vehicle.

With everybody and everything in place, now they were finally on their way. It seemed as if the ride took a long time, but it was only a twelve-minute drive. By now, it was 11:00 p.m.

The staff were awaiting their arrival. They greeted them at the entry and immediately commenced the process.

When the doctor completed the initial examination, he determined the baby would make his entry very soon. Mom was quickly whisked to delivery, and the nine-month wait was finally completed.

In the calm and peaceful atmosphere at the center, a healthy baby boy was born. They had previously chosen a name for him.

LIVE FAST *before your clock strikes* 12

When Mom and Dad held him, they looked in his face and said, "Welcome to the world, Dran."

As he was making his entry to the world, the downtown clock's *bong* could be heard. They all could hear a muffled echo through the mountains. They acknowledged the midnight sound and laughed that Dran was born on the cusp of a new day.

And then, the strangest thing happened. Lights began to flicker rapidly. The building had a huge vibration as if there were an earthquake. The darkness of the night dissipated, and the sky shone as bright as a noonday sun. There seemed to be some major commotion going on in the atmosphere.

There was shock and awe within the center. No one could explain what had just happened. This happened at a critical time. The medical center began to put backup systems in place for this new baby and the many patients at the center. Within a matter of twelve minutes, things were back to normal. The sun disappeared, and the darkness reappeared in the sky. Now the team put their full attention directly on the new baby Dran.

Many of the staff came to see the new baby. They were puzzled about what had happened, but they were glad to see he was OK. Their focus had been to assist in bringing a healthy baby into the world. That feat had been accomplished. Whatever happened did not interfere with their duties and care. They wondered, and some discussed, whether this birth could have contributed to what they had witnessed. The instability of the atmosphere and the vibrations at the medical center were a true mystery.

They continued to meet the needs of the baby and his family, and after three days, they were discharged to go home. Dran's family was ready to start their lives together.

While they were riding home, they traveled through downtown Gua. As they approached the clock, Dran's father glimpsed up toward the sky. He was once again startled to see the image of the same bear in the clouds. He did not utter a word, but he knew for sure that the bear was a significant symbol in their lives.

There was some normalcy at home, but it was also foreign territory to have a new baby in their midst. They were all learning from one another. There were times that when the baby cried, they wanted to cry also. Because that was not a viable solution, they continued to do their best to take care of Dran. They would know what they needed when they needed to know.

Dran was very observant, even as a small baby. He was a prime example of an exceptional and advanced child. He portrayed advanced cognitive skills that exuded atypical intelligence. Other people would acknowledge he was a child beyond his years.

His parents did not always know the milestone markers of what he should be doing. However, they were fully aware that he was exceeding many of the norms. He was doing exceptional feats at an incredibly early age.

LIVE FAST before your clock strikes 12

From the Thoughts of Dran

I am an example of what it means to live life fast. I was born as a small baby. My weight was under six pounds. Guess I was trying to hurry and get here to get on with the show. I was a long and wrinkly little fellow with many crevices to fill out. My doctor even insightfully revealed that based on my body and muscle structure, I would be a large man. That was encouraging to my parents to know that even though I was small, I was healthy and well.

I felt a little bit on display when so many people came to see me. I wondered what they were thinking when they saw me. There were times I wished I could say "boo" and scare them away. Sometimes I would hear some of the well-wishers say funny things in weird voices. It would make me smile and laugh. Too bad I could not talk back to them. Sometimes though, I brought out an approving belch and hiccups.

One of my well-wishers brought a big box over for me as a welcome gift for my arrival. The box was covered in beautiful blue paper with polka dots over the entire sheet. I was fascinated with the bright paper. It did not concern me as to what was in the box. That box and paper had my full attention. Mom placed me on her lap to encourage me to open it and see the contents. We could go through the box together. She let me pull all the wrappings off strip by strip. I loved the rattling of the paper. I was having so much fun. Finally, all the paper was gone, and it was time to open the box. There were diapers, clothes, and a toy rattle. At the very bottom of the box, I felt something soft. It was a beautiful stuffed animal. It was a furry, brown grizzly bear. Finally, something I could enjoy! I forgot all about the box, and with the biggest smile, I pulled it toward me. I jumped from Momma's lap, and I gave that bear a big hug. It felt as if the bear hugged me back. The bear and I had a special bond, and he immediately became my best friend. They were all thrilled to see how much I loved the bear. I gave him the name Benno. It seemed that the

LIVE FAST before your clock strikes 12

name fit my new friend. From that day on, Benno was with me day and night. He even slept with me in my crib. I loved him, and Benno loved me.

I spent most of my baby time lying around. Most people would describe it as crying, eating, and of course, pooping. However, I beg to differ. I was instead strategizing how to get out of that crib and gain my freedom. After all, I had places to go. I needed to explore. From where I was lying, there was a lot out there for me to see and do.

While I was strategizing, there were others making plans for me. I had no doubt they had my best interests in mind, but only a few of our plans were the same. Someone was in store for a shocking surprise.

I certainly enjoyed the meals I was getting, and it showed. All those wrinkles and crevices filled up quickly. Among my family, I became known as that "fat baby boy, double chin and all."

People would often make comments about me learning to do things fast. They would say, he must be getting out of the way for the next one. I guess it was their way of hinting that I needed a playmate. Nevertheless, I did not allow it to deter me from figuring out my next move.

Days and weeks went by, and I was getting fatter and taller.

Benno and I were getting into so many mischievous things. I had a partner in crime. Sometimes I restrained myself, because I did not want Benno to be taken from me. When we got in trouble, Benno had to go to time-out. That was the worst punishment for me. It would make me incredibly sad. I did my best to keep this from happening, but it happened more times than I care to remember.

I learned to crawl very quickly. I could move in and out without much notice from others. I even learned to turn around in close quarters. The question was often asked, how did I get there that fast? It seemed as if I had sneakers on my knees.

I observed that I could cause people to smile when I said or did certain things. That caused me to crave more of that laughter. Just maybe that was part of my purpose. Just maybe I was gifted to bring joy in others' lives. I did not have it all figured out, but I would just keep doing what I was doing and wait and see what would happen.

One day, I was sitting in my toddler rocking chair. I was supposed to watch one of the cartoons. As I sat in the chair, I saw a clear path to the back door. While Mom was washing clothes in the laundry room, I made my great escape. The kitchen door was propped open, so I pushed it wider. When I looked out the door, I ran into my first challenge. There were steps!!

With Benno in my hand, I turned around slowly and backed down the steps with little effort. Wow; I impressed myself! When my feet hit the ground, the dirt felt very strange to me. I had never felt the dirt before.

My next challenge became, I wonder what it tastes like. So, I grabbed a handful and placed it right in my mouth. I found out

LIVE FAST before your clock strikes 12

in short order that it was a major mistake. It was not a favorable experience. I spit it out and looked to see what else was available for me to try. As I was approaching my next experience, I heard a very loud scream. Momma was calling my name. I could hear the stomping of her feet getting closer to me. Suddenly fear overtook me, and I knew I had done something very wrong.

"Dran! Dran! Dran! Where are you?" Momma said.

I answered, very meekly, "Ooh." That was the only sound I could make.

She ran toward me, scooped me up, and held me tight. She then jerked me around and pried open my stiff mouth. She took her finger and felt around to see if I had anything lodged in my mouth or throat. There was nothing there. I could sense her relief.

She began to tell me in a relieved voice that I should not do that again. I frightened her, and she emphasized that I could have hurt myself.

I held onto Benno tight, and I started to cry. I did not like seeing my Momma upset and clearly understood the danger I put myself and Benno in.

In a soft whispering voice, she said, "Dran, you must learn to wait on others to help you sometimes. Stop trying to do it all on your own."

As sincere as she was, I must admit, it mostly went in one ear and out the other.

I needed to continue exploring, and I did not have time to waste.

* * *

The goal for his parents was to see Dran thrive in every area of his life. They wanted him to learn to be independent yet always know they were never far away. They would allow him to be a problem-solver without their interference.

There was always free time to explore and be creative with a balance of having chores and responsibilities. It was astonishing to see his development and watch him become the person he was meant to be.

There were realistic expectations for his behavior. They would often offer explanations and reasons why the rules applied in a particular situation, but there were real consequences for unfavorable behavior. It was important to them to have consistency.

They would always take Dran's concerns seriously, and he was allowed to express his feelings respectfully and freely. He felt that he was loved, nurtured, and supported by them. He felt protected.

His parents were his biggest encouragers. They would praise the positive things that Dran was doing and encourage him to keep up the clever work. They were encouraged by many of the neighbors when they praised Dran's behavior too. His interaction with them exemplified obvious solid home training. This reinforced the things they were trying to instill in him.

LIVE FAST *before your clock strikes* 12

Dran's parents interacted with him, playing games, doing bike rides, reading, and watching movies. There was always plenty of discussion about what they did or saw. Opinions were always heard and respected.

It was a high priority to them that they demonstrated moral and spiritual responsibility. Dran's parents were empathetic toward others and taught Dran to be. They often did charitable events together throughout the area of Gua.

Since their family was such a strong presence in the animal community, they had consistently practiced compassionate acts during Dran's life.

Siblings

Their small family unit of three was fine-tuned and running smoothly, and then Dran's first sibling came along. When she arrived, the dynamics changed. The parents now had to divide time addressing the needs of each child. They noticed some jealousy going on for a while, and then they began to see the much-desired sibling bond developing.

It did not take long for Dran to find himself nestled with three female siblings. He often wondered how he was so fortunate to be surrounded by these beautiful and intelligent young ladies.

Later, he understood how they would continuously play such a vital role in his life. In time, he finally realized that he gained a wealth of knowledge from them that could never be taught at a university. He would like to believe they learned a thing or two from him as well.

The parents then acknowledged the individual needs of each child. They strived extremely hard to fulfill them. There was no lack of praise and encouragement available. They recognized the unique differences in their personalities and found it interesting as to how well they complemented one another. As a family, there was still a strong, cohesive unit. They cherished their time together. The love of their family comforted and reassured one another.

Their family became a model in the community. Many observers embodied all these strong qualities that they witnessed. Other children in the community would flock to their home to enjoy the magnetic atmosphere of Dran's household.

The outside influences did not penetrate the layer of protection that was established through their love. They exposed them to life that equipped them to think and act for themselves.

The parents considered it an honor to raise and nurture the four siblings. They had the privilege and responsibility to shape a young life. They gleamed at the healthy development into their adulthood, knowing that future generations would have their contribution for many years to come.

The multifaceted role of parents carries enormous potential or great disaster. Dran's parents embraced their role with confidence, believing their children would be great contributors to society.

EMPHASIZED DIFFERENCES DISPELLED

THERE HAVE BEEN MANY WARS IN THE WORLD FOUGHT because of differences. The ideas of superiority and rules are often magnified because of exalted egos.

There is a story about two families who dwelled together on a one-hundred-acre farm. It was considered one of the best and most well-kept pieces of property in the county. However, there were distinct differences in the lives of each family.

The owner's family spent their days in shops, decorating the house, and eating delicacy foods from imported markets. They traveled throughout the world on numerous vacations. They wore tailor-made clothes and custom shoes. Their children attended private schools and were privileged with school boarding. They prided themselves on being the elite portion of society and cherished the fact that they were different.

They hosted many events on the property, but the servant family was never invited to attend. They did not mingle with the servant family outside of work-related occurrences.

They never shared any of their goods with the servant family because they did not want their lives to be compared. They would not even share hand-me-down clothing or leftover foods. The servants were instructed to give all leftover food to the animals. They did not want the servant family to develop an appetite for the finer things in life. They did not want to risk the servants believing they were in the same financial status. They wanted to remind them consistently that they were different.

The servant family of fifteen lived on one hundred acres but were confined to two houses. They were required to pay rent even though they took care of the land.

They shopped at the local market on Friday after their weekly stipend. They often made their own clothes because of the limited income.

Each day the servants would arise and resume their previous workday duties. It involved tending the farm animals, which included milking, gathering, and feeding. They provided all the labor to keep the farm functioning at its peak.

The servant family often spoke among themselves of their desire to own their own homes where they could have more space. They were dissatisfied with being dependent on the owner's family. In addition, they were often not spoken to nicely because the owners had considered them different.

The difference between the two families was only subject to financial status. That was what allowed for such a variation of experiences. Nothing about them stood out so differently that they could not share some of their lives together.

Early one Friday morning, the servant family started their workday before dawn. It was a day scheduled for plowing a vegetable garden. It was predicted to be hot later that day, so the servants wanted to finish early. They always looked forward to the weekend to have private family time and enjoyment.

As the plowing began, the plow only completed two rows, and the blade hit a hard piece in the soil. Upon investigation, they saw it was a lockbox buried in the ground.

The servant family took the box home without sharing any information with the owners about what they found.

There was not a key, so when they get home, they pried the locked box open. No one could prepare them for what they found in the box. There were detailed letters that exposed a dark history between the two families. The owners were unknowingly a part of deception from five generations. The owners were not aware of crimes committed by their ancestors in previous years.

The servant's ancestors had been true owners of the property the entire time. They were the rightful owners of the one hundred acres.

The owner's ancestral family had brought harm to the servant's ancestral family many years ago. It happened because the servant's ancestral family would not sell their property for a deflated price. Instead, a fake land transfer deed was drawn, and a forged signature was done to complete the deceptive transaction.

The owner's ancestors allowed the servant ancestors to remain on the property as laborers. It was also their way of keeping the secret confined.

The big lie had been perpetuated for five generations, but it was finally being exposed.

The servant family sought legal assistance from a renowned law firm who specialized in land restitution. It was proven through the court system that the servant family were in fact the true owners of the one hundred acres.

The court allowed a ninety-day window for the owner's family to relocate or negotiate a deal with the servant family to remain as tenants on the property.

To make the situation right, the servant family offered an exchange to allow the owner family to move into the two houses for the same rental amount and work on the land as they had done for the last four generations. They could now see firsthand what being labeled different really felt like.

The owner's family began to recognize the error of their ways, but they could not bring themselves to accept the servant's family offer. Instead, they relocated to a state completely across the country where no one would know their story.

The emphasis on the difference had left no room for compromise. The loss outweighed the gain.

There had always been a way to live at peace with one another, but using differences as the adhesive to mend the ego destroyed what could have been a harmonic and respectful life.

Instead, the cancerous exposure of difference and deceit festered until it ruptured. Only then could healing finally become possible.

The servant family had now become the owner family with the vow to never let differences dictate their love and concern for humanity.

There are obvious differences that cannot and should not be denied.

Society has, however, encouraged human beings to be psychologically hardwired to fear differences. Instead of curiosity, it is suspicion and despisal.

This exacerbated action contributed to the psychology of tribalism.

Tumultuous years have been wasted with never-ending research on emphasized differences.

The fabric that knits us together has been pulled at the seam. A continuing unraveling has distorted the shape of a well-constructed society.

We have the benefit of shared experiences of awe, humor, and physical exertion to help transcend our differences.

We have a society full of technology that makes it possible to connect people instantly throughout the world.

The same technology that connects us compounds our divisional instincts.

In the upcoming pages, a story of Reb and Dran's lives will evolve to uncover many correlations. The kinship of life's experience is applicable to all of life. Their common denominators become obvious as they maneuver the various stages of their lives.

Their lives become surprisingly interchangeable ,and despite the obvious differences, they overcome life's obstacles. The two become one and the same.

LIFE OF REB AND DRAN:
00:01 A.M. TO 06:00 A.M.

Reb and His Innocent Trouble

Growing up in the forest as a bear cub brought about many challenges.

There were predators and prey throughout the woodland. There were those that hunt and those that were hunted. Reb quickly became aware that depending on his most current situation, he encountered being in both of those roles at any given time.

Even with their impressive size and strength, it was burdensome to avoid testings. If it were a confrontation, there was a strong chance that he would win, but the efforts were mentally exhausting. The environment, the other animals, and human-bear conflict were just a few of the demands. There were territory disputes even from another bear. They were confronted with mating battles, which was also commonplace.

One of the toughest tasks was choosing the appropriate skill to use in an instant. There was always no time to waste. The response you made could be life-threatening. You must think fast in the forest. Many obstacles required a knowledge of unique skills to maneuver and survive.

Their dwindling population due to hunting and habitat loss was a constant reminder of their vulnerability. They strived for protection to overcome the many challenges they were facing.

Many other animals had stereotypes and prejudices about bears. For example, many of the animals believed that because bears had hibernation seasons, bears were extremely lazy. This was, however, along with other misnomers, far from true. Reb and others had strong convictions that the bear community were some of the most intelligent animals in the forest.

He focused on his strengths and continued to get stronger. He was clumsy, but he could move fast.

He could not see or hear very well due to the lack of development of his senses. But one of the keener senses was that of smell, and he was good at that. He could smell food from a mile away.

Reb knew that he needed to learn fast, because his time with Mom was limited. She had informed him that he would eventually have to become independent, living on his own. She encouraged him to pay close attention to the things she was doing to help him survive. Reb was confident, however, that when that time came, he would be ready. His mom would assure that.

Reb's climbing skills were impressive. He had practiced and built strength and confidence. His sharp claws provided just the grip he needed to hold tight while he made his way up a tree. Climbing was something Reb genuinely enjoyed, and many other animals often complimented him on his skills. It was just one of the things that made Reb unique.

One day, Reb had been placed in a tree by his mother. She had chosen one of the strongest tree limbs to secure him in place. She went out for food for the day. Her instruction was, "Reb, please stay in the tree until I return to take you back to the den." The greatest reward for Reb was enjoying the food she would return with for dinner. He could envision the salmon and honey she would bring for a healthy and delicious meal. Mom even suggested they make it a special meal. They could celebrate Reb staying on his own for the first time in the forest. Mom began her foraging with confidence that Reb would be on that tree branch when she returned.

As soon as she left on her hunting mission, Reb put his plan into action. He wanted to test his skills to see if he knew as much as he thought he knew. He began to inch down the tree. He was thinking and saying aloud, "I can get back before Mom returns. She will never know about my little escapade."

Though he knew the tree was for his protection from the animals, he felt prepared to face whatever he confronted in the forest. Wow, was he wrong.

No sooner did Reb's paw touch the ground than he sensed something creeping in his presence. He thought, "Maybe Mom is returning." If she were, he would be in big trouble. If it was not Mom, he may be in even bigger trouble.

When he glimpsed it from the corner of his eye, he realized it was not Mom.

Instead, it was a large cougar, tiptoeing toward him, preparing for the pounce. The cougar had conducted enough surveillance to know that Reb was alone. Reb was still not big enough for the cougar to feel any type of genuine threat. Therefore, he was willing to take his chances.

Reb bellied up a small whimper. He could barely get it out because of the fear wrenching his body. He knew he was at the mercy of this hungry cougar.

This was one time that he hoped his mom would hear him and come back to save him. Maybe she would finish her foraging early and hurry back to get him. After all, that cougar would dare not tackle his large sow mom.

Reb did not know much about the life of a cougar, but he surmised that the cougar was older and more mature than him. From his mom's teaching, he knew that cougars typically do not eat bears, but they may if they are hungry. They also may need to feed their litter. If that were the case, they would settle for whatever meat they could find. Reb's thinking was that the cougar would much rather eat a deer or mountain goat. There were many other preferred dishes other than a bear. But he knew he could not convince a hungry cougar. Through his mom's training, he also knew they were both predators and not natural enemies. He knew the cougar had no venom, but they both had sharp claws and teeth.

To get away fast, Reb scurried up the tree. He was quick, and he was careful not to slip and fall in the space of the cougar. He used his razor-sharp claws to defend and to climb.

At one point, the cougar made eye contact with Reb. Reb's eyesight was still not great, but it was well enough to see the tenacity in the cougar. Reb trembled profusely. He was terrified.

He attempted to do a bluff charge, with his head and ears up and forward. This puff made him look bigger. Though it was meant to intimidate, it had an insignificant effect on the determined cougar. The response from the cougar was an aggressive posture and a sharp hissing sound. It was enough to let Reb know he was in extreme danger.

There was nothing else Reb could do, therefore, Reb accepted the inevitable destiny as to what would happen next. He was on the verge of his demise.

As fate would have it, the large branch he had been sitting on delivered a loud crack. Apparently, it had not been strong enough after all. It plummeted from the tree and came crashing right between Reb and the cougar. The noise was startling for them both. They both thought it was a gunshot from a human. Reb jumped from the tree in one move, and the cougar used his agility to make a quick turn. They began to run as fast as they could in opposite directions. They had both narrowly escaped serious harm from the impact of the branch. Neither looked back but used their skills to get out of harm's way.

Talk about a miraculous turn of events! They had both experienced one.

After a brief time of waiting, Reb thought it was safe to head back to the tree. He wanted to make sure that no additional branches would fall. Surely Mom would be back soon, and he needed to be in place. He made his way back to the tree, huffing and puffing, but he mustered up enough strength to climb up in the tree and nestle himself on another large, strong branch. It was bigger than the branch where his mom placed him.

As he was climbing, he was thinking, "That was a close call, and I would never do that again." He had barely escaped. There had been double jeopardy from the cougar and from the tree branch. He lay on the branch, reflecting on all the things that had just happened.

When Reb's mom returned with the food, he was ecstatic to see her. He was also happy to see the delicious food. He greeted her with big hugs and kisses. She could not remember Reb ever being so excited and affectionate. She thought that he must really be hungry and happy to see the food she brought him. She knew he was hoping for salmon and honey, and she had delivered just what he wanted. She was equally happy to see Reb still nestled on the tree branch, waiting for her return.

Reb could not bring himself to share what had happened. He did not want her to lose all trust in his ability to be obedient to her instructions. He knew that Mom would express her disappointment and he would really feel bad that he hurt her. In addition, he would hear a long lecture on their walk back home.

After weighing out the pros and cons of telling her, he decided that this incident should remain a secret between him and the cougar. He knew the cougar would not tell.

The path home was usually quiet, but this time, the quietness brought about an eeriness. Reb still had jitters from his ordeal. Each ruffle of the leaves caused his heart to beat faster.

He was thinking that the cougar might startle them by jumping from a tree directly in their path. After all, he knew the capabilities of the cougar. He had just witnessed him in action.

His fears were soon calmed when he remembered he was now with Mom. He began to walk closer to her. He was so close that he almost tripped her a few times. She reminded him to walk with a little more space between them.

When he finally glimpsed the den, he ran ahead of her and waited by the entry. He was glad to be home. She even said to him, "Reb, you must really be starving."

When they sat down for their evening meal, Reb was thinking, "This is the most delicious meal ever, and I almost missed it." He ate all that Mom Sow had prepared.

Mom Sow did not know what happened at the tree, but she sensed there was something he was not sharing.

She thought, "And by the way, he was not on the same branch I placed him on. I wonder why?"

Dran and Benno

Dran was living out the predictions from his birth doctor. He had seen the potential in Dran even though he was a small baby. He had observed the broad shoulders and the long limbs and knew this was the frame of a large man. Dran was certainly on his way to proving this to be true. He had grown physically as well as portrayed mental maturity.

When Dran thought of his future, he saw himself as a strong, competent man. He could envision himself as a man of stature in both physical and intellectual characteristics. He saw himself doing good in the world. The doctor could predict his physical size, but the doctor could not predict the size of his heart or his desires. This was being birthed from within.

He would observe his dad and other men that he admired. He had been fortunate enough to meet his maternal grandfather and his maternal great-grandfather. They radiated love and kindness, which were traits he desired to emulate. Though he was still young in comparison to them, they were examples of men he wanted to pattern his life after.

By now, Dran had a sister. He had not been overly excited when she arrived in the household, but over time, he learned to love her immensely. It was as if she had always been a part of his life. They were siblings, but they also became friends.

It was their parents' dream to have loving children who cared for one another. They saw the close bond being established between the two of them, and it brought them all boundless joy. They were learning the importance of sharing and cooperating. They did not always see eye-to-eye, but they always compromised, and things worked out. It showed that they were both maturing.

Dran's parents realized he was close to his sister when he would often let his sister play with Benno. He had to trust someone deeply to allow them to play with Benno. Dran had no problem if she asked his permission. He knew Benno was safe with her. He considered her to be an excellent bear sitter. They had some memorable times with the three of them playing together.

When Dran started preschool, he was quickly recognized as being mature for his age. He found his place in the role of becoming a dependable teacher helper in the classroom.

There were many eventful days during their school years. Mom and Dad took lots of pictures as keepsakes. They kept a scrapbook to share with the children when they got older. They might not remember all the details, but the pictures would be valuable in helping to remember time and place.

School was so much fun for Dran. He looked forward each day to spending time with his friends. The days were filled with adventure, and he was anxious to go home in the evening to share with his parents. He was equally excited to compare stories with his sister. The stories would continue to build all week, and Friday was the climax. Friday was a day of show-and-tell. Each student brought in something that they would share as they stood before the class.

Dran tried to think of something to take to school with him. What could he talk about? His sister decided to take a pink cap and explain to the class why it was her favorite. She loved her pink hat almost as much as Dran loved Benno. She had been known to sleep in her pink hat on more than one occasion.

After much pondering, Dran decided to take Benno. Benno had never been to school before.

His parents questioned Dran as to whether he thought this would be a clever idea. But Dran wanted his friends to finally meet Benno, whom he talked about so much. They all agreed, and he assured them he would be extra careful and take loving care of Benno.

He put him in his backpack, and off to school they went. He would periodically feel his backpack to make sure he was still in there. He was so excited to share, but he did not know where to

LIVE FAST before your clock strikes 12

start. There was so much to talk about when it came to his friend Benno.

When it was time for Dran's presentation, he reached into his bag to pull out Benno. He had been in there all day, so he was crunched up pretty badly. The children laughed at him, which really hurt Dran's feelings, but he was still happy to share. They all really loved hearing Dran's story. Dran even passed Benno around and let them say hello and touch Benno. When Dran finished his presentation, his friends gave him and Benno a rousing round of applause.

It had all gone well, and Dran could not wait to share all the details when he got home.

At 12:00 naptime, Dran was happy that he had Benno at school to sleep with him. He went comfortably to sleep with Benno close by his side.

When naptime was finished, Dran was sleeping so hard that he did not hear his name called. His teacher had called loudly, but to no avail. When the noise from the other students persisted, Dran finally woke up. He had slept so comfortably with Benno.

The rest of the day was busy as the other children finished their presentations.

At last, the school bell rang; Dran grabbed his backpack and ran to the line to get on the bus. He laughed and talked with his friends until the bus stopped at his house. Dran said goodbye to everyone and jumped off to run home. They would see each other on Monday. He and his sister ran to the house together. They would take turns sharing, but they needed to decide who would go first. The one who ran home first would be the winner. It was Dran's sister.

When they got inside, she immediately started to tell the story of the pink hat. Her friends at school really loved hearing about all the places she had worn it. She found out that one of her friends had one just like it in a yellow color. They said they would dress alike and wear them on the same day. She enjoyed sharing this story with her family, and they were glad her show-and-tell had been such a success.

Now it was Dran's turn. He opened his backpack, and to his dismay, Benno was gone. Dran screamed at the top of his voice. Mom knew something was terribly wrong. Once she found out Benno was missing, she tried to comfort Dran. She also called the school to ask them to be on the lookout for Benno.

They were closing for the weekend, and no one had turned Benno in at the office.

Dran wished he had never taken Benno to school, and he could not believe he had left him.

For some consolation, Mom walked outside with him to search the area from the bus stop.

He could have fallen from the backpack when he and his sister were running home.

There were no signs of Benno.

Dran began to wonder if he would ever see Benno again.

His sister tried to encourage him to play, but he was not the least bit interested.

His only focus was on seeing Benno again.

When it was time for dinner, he had no appetite, so he went to his room, laid down, and cried himself to sleep.

He woke up thinking this was a bad dream. Once he realized it was not a dream, he accepted it was his worst nightmare. All he could think to do was pace the floor back and forth. He knew it would not get him anywhere, but it gave him something to do.

When he was tired of doing that, he walked out on the porch and then made his way to the tree in the yard. He leaned against the tree trunk for a while. Then he slid down to the ground, where he lay prostrate, looking into the sky. He apologized to Benno for losing him. He hoped he was okay, wherever he was. He eventually nodded off to sleep while he was outside.

Dran's parents thought he was still in his room, so Dad went to check on him. To his surprise, Dran was not there. He called out Dran's name but got no response. Then the search began. The entire family was looking for Dran. The noise woke Dran up. He jumped up and ran toward the porch at the same time they were running outside. They almost collided with one another. What a relief it was to know Dran was okay. Dad said to him, "We cannot lose you and Benno on the same day." Dran agreed and apologized. They all went back inside for the night.

When they got inside, they sat at the table and talked about what they could do. They could find another stuffed bear similar to Benno. But Dran knew Benno could never be replaced. Nevertheless, he agreed to go shopping. That might help him calm down.

Just as they were finishing the conversation, the doorbell rang.

Dad went to the door to see who was in that unfamiliar car. It was Dran's teacher.

She walked to the door, carrying a shopping bag in her hands.

"Hi there," she said. "It is getting late, but I wanted to bring this to Dran. When he did show-and-tell today, he shared how much little Benno means to him. I could not bear to see him go through the weekend without his good friend." She just knew she had to get Benno back home.

Dran heard his teacher's voice. He ran to the door and saw the bag in her hand. "Dran," said his mom. "Someone wants to see you."

He reached to give his teacher a big hug. "Thank you so much," Dran said.

He reached for the bag and grabbed Benno. He gave him a big hug too.

Everyone in the house was smiling. Benno was finally home.

Dran could now eat. He suddenly had an appetite.

After he ate, he and his sister played with Benno.

LIVE FAST *before your clock strikes* **12**

At bedtime, Dran tucked Benno in the bed first. He whispered to him, "This is your first and last day of school." He then crawled into the bed and went fast asleep, holding hands with Benno.

He still got the chance to go shopping, but he left Benno at home.

6:00 a.m. Encounter at the Animal Reserve

Gua was a fortunate city to have so many species of animals. The wildlife area off Forest Road was a popular tour for visitors to the city. It flourished as the premier territory for preservation of undomesticated animals and birds in their native habitat.

Dran's father had served as an advisor to keep the reservation with excellent standards. They had been the recipient of several national awards. Many delegates had traveled there from other parts of the world to observe the methods used to operate such a proficient reserve. They would later apply that knowledge to the habitat in their area with the hopes of major improvements.

There had been a collaboration of the park officials and the school board to expand the reserve exposure to the students. They created a guided-tour series to allow this unique experience for the children while assuring the animals stayed safe.

This was the inaugural year for the first school trip. Up until now, parents would take their children on individual outings there, but they were limited to animal exposure. Some exhibits were not open. Therefore, there were many animals that the children had not seen. Now the exhibits and displays had been expanded and it would be a more detailed experience.

Everyone in the community seemed excited for the children. Even the news reporters were preparing to make this a major news story when the day arrived.

Because of the overwhelming interest, the school was requesting parent volunteers to assist the teachers as chaperones. It was one of the ways the school was designing a plan to assure everything flowed smoothly. The primary grades were the initial group for the trip. Dran was one of the fortunate ones that was part of that group.

Dran was hoping one or both of his parents could volunteer. He thought it would be fun to share this experience with them.

He had brought the consent form home several days ago, yet his parents had not said anything about the trip to him. He wanted them to hurry with his form, because there was a deadline and a capacity limit. He was hoping that the delay was because they were deciding if either of them would join him.

What a pleasant surprise it was when he got home from school. His mom had signed the paper and had placed it in an envelope. That feeling proved short-lived when she informed him that neither she nor Dad would be able to attend because of prior work commitments. They had tried to work it out, but things had not fallen in place. Even though that brought some disappointment, Dran gladly accepted the signed paper and tucked it securely in his backpack.

There were exactly twelve days (about one week and five days) before the trip. They knew it would be difficult to keep Dran contained, so Mom made a countdown calendar for Dran. She hung it on the refrigerator door as a constant reminder that the time was moving fast.

Every morning, he would grab his red crayon and put a big X mark around the day. It was twenty-four hours closer to his trip.

In class, they had been discussing all the animals they might see. His teacher had them bring in a picture of their favorite animal. He took a picture of Benno; after all, he was by far his favorite animal. He had told Benno all about the trip. He wished he could take him in his backpack, but he had had such a traumatic experience before. He would not dare risk losing him again.

On the day before the trip, Dran helped his mother pack his lunch box and an extra snack. After dinner, he begged to go to bed early. He was ready for bed as soon as it got dark outside. She agreed, and he was in bed by 7:00 p.m. He knew that as soon as he woke up, it would be time to get ready for school. Then his day of adventure would be here. It took a while, but he went to sleep after a few tosses and turns.

At 6:00 a.m., the alarm clock went off, and Dran jumped right out of bed. He even got to the clock before Mom. He hurried to get dressed, eat, and grab his belongings. By 6:45 a.m., he was standing by the door, waiting to exit.

He was excited that Mom and Dad were both taking him to school, even though they could not make the bus ride to the animal park.

While riding to school, there were more discussions about the animals they would see at the reservation. He was making the sounds of animals and even had Mom and Dad make some sounds too. They played a guessing game of "Who am I?" Dran was the winner hands down.

Soon they were pulling up in the school parking lot. There were four buses waiting. Parents, teachers, and students filled the school yard. There were people everywhere. Mom and Dad wished they were going to help, because it looked like they could use extra hands. But they knew Dran was safe and would have lots of fun.

Dran gave a big hug, and off he went to join the other students. He was assigned a seat about midway on the bus. He was content, because he was sitting beside his best friend. They had a lovely view inside the bus and all the outside scenes.

The children had been encouraged to wear something with an animal emblem. They could wear a shirt, pants, socks, and shoes, but no hats. The hats would be too distracting and hard to keep up with. Dran wore a sweater with a picture of a big bear on the front. It reminded him of Benno. Since he did not have him, a picture would be the next best thing. He would just pretend to allow the animals to meet his best friend.

The ride was about one hour long. On the way there, they sang songs about animals, and there was even a video for them to watch. This helped the time go quickly, and before they knew it, they arrived at the reservation. There was a hush over the bus. The excitement was overwhelming with the young students. One of the teachers broke the silence by screaming loudly, "We are here." The students responded with a loud, "Yeah."

This marked the beginning of the adventures.

When they arrived, there were animal billboards lining the gates. The signs had all the animals he hoped to see. This made it even more thrilling; they were finally here. A big grizzly bear was the largest picture of all. It stood out from among all the other animals. It would be his dream to see the real one inside the gates. It would be the highlight of his day.

The groups were divided into groups of five. The teachers and chaperones took their places, and off they went to start this exciting adventure.

The property was many acres of land. The animals were fortunate to have the large property to roam freely. It was a natural environment for the animals. There were trees and lakes to make the animals feel right at home.

As they began their walk with the tour guide, many exciting details were given about the animals' life. They were allowed to ask questions to find out more if they liked. Each exhibit had a limited stay so that other groups could follow.

From Dran's observation, the animals seemed happy and looked like they were having fun. Because they were not in cages, it was a little difficult to keep up with them. They were moving around extremely fast.

The design of the reserve prioritized safety. There were trenches and barriers, along with glass partitions, to keep the children and the animals apart from one another.

Dran saw gorillas, zebras, and the mighty lions, all of which were on his list of animals he hoped to see. He also saw alligators and manatees in the water.

Each animal Dran saw brought such exhilaration. His heartbeat pounded so fast through his shirt that it looked as if the bear on his shirt was jumping.

The animals were huge. They towered so far over him that he stretched his neck and stood on his toes to see some of them. He was happy that they had glass between them. It made him feel more comfortable not being so close.

The group made their way to the bear exhibit. This was the exhibit that Dran was looking forward to seeing most. There they were. There were several bears of all sizes. There were grizzlies, black bears, brown bears, sloth bears, and pandas. There were not any polar bears, which was a little disappointing, but Dran was accepting of that. He had studied the bears in detail, and he could recognize them by sight. He even knew right away that Benno was in the grizzly bear family. It dawned on him that if Benno were as big as his cousin, he would not be able to live in the same house with him.

This was Dran's favorite exhibit. The guide was able to share more insight into the life of a bear, and Dran enjoyed all the details. He was so surprised to see some of them stand and walk on two legs. They walked as proficiently as a human, and they could run over thirty miles per hour on two legs. He did not have a camera, but he had a great photographic memory. He would be able to describe the bears in detail to his family.

LIVE FAST before your clock strikes 12

Dran was so mesmerized by the bears. He just stared and smiled. One of the grizzly cubs reminded him of Benno. They had remarkably similar noses and eyes. While looking at him, Dran saw the cub look directly back at him. He really thought that he smiled and winked, but he did not want to tell that to anyone. The cub ran down a path but quickly turned around and returned to the same spot, still looking directly at Dran. The cub stood up on two legs and turned around in a circle as if it was a dance. He then lay in the grass, still with his eyes fixed on Dran.

Dran's teacher noticed the cub being very playful with Dran. All the students also noticed the special attention the bear was paying to Dran. The guide said that out of the many tours he had done, he had never seen the bear acting like that before. They wondered if it was the shirt Dran was wearing, or was it something more mystical? It was obvious that there was something that brought a connection to Dran and that bear.

When it was time to move to the next exhibit, Dran really did not want to go. He wished he could spend more time with the bear. That bear cub really did like him, and he liked the little bear cub. He decided to give him a special name. He named him Bruno. It was a name that rhymed with Benno. He liked the way it sounded together. If only he had little Benno with him. He was sure they would really like one another. Maybe his parents could bring him and his sister back to the reserve. He could bring Benno with him to meet his newfound cousin.

He moved on to the next exhibit and saw a mountain lion. He was interesting to look at, but his mind was on the previous exhibit with the bear. In fact, he really did not hear much of what the guide said from that point on.

Pretty soon, they were at the end of the exhibits. Time had gone by fast for the children because they were having so much fun. The final stop was the reserve gift shop. The children were allowed to go into the gift shop, where they could purchase souvenirs. There were many items, and some were miniature versions of the things and animals they had seen.

Dran knew exactly what he wanted to buy. He headed straight to the bear section. He wanted to find a small version of the bear he had connected with. He could not find it, so he purchased two bear keychains for Mom and Dad, two bear coloring books for him and his sister, and a bear sticker for Benno.

On the bus ride back to the school, all that Dran thought about was that bear. He needed to convince his parents to take him out there for a family visit. He did not talk much with his friends on the bus, because his mind was distracted.

It was about 6:00 p.m. when they arrived back at school. Dad and Mom were there to greet him. They could see that Dran was excited, but they also sensed that he was fatigued. Those things were true for Dran, but he could not rest until he shared the story of the bear. He began telling his parents the story, and he talked nonstop all the way home. He was barely taking breaths between

LIVE FAST before your clock strikes 12

sentences. He finally worked his conversation to the major question at hand: Would they please take him back to the reserve to see Bruno? He wanted to take his sister, and of course Benno, to meet his new friend.

Dad explained that if they returned to the reserve, he might not see the same bear. They did not stay in the same place but roamed throughout the habitat.

Dran was ready to take that chance. He knew that when he returned, the bear would find him.

Dad and Mom agreed to have a family outing soon at the animal reserve.

Dran could not be happier. When he got home, he gave out the gifts from the gift shop.

He realized that he was extremely tired, so he ate, showered, and went to bed.

Dran rested well that night. He dreamed about the bear.

VIVIAN WARD NEWTON

It's 6:00 a.m.

Reb and Dran were born
at an exciting time and place.
They had some great adventures
as they hustled to keep pace
here, there, and everywhere,
often running into roadblocks.
But they had to do it quickly.
Oh no! It's six o'clock!

A Time of Beginning and Growth
Attributes at 00:01 a.m. to 6:00 a.m.

From conception to the planting of a fertilized egg and birth, life begins.

Initially there is not much to do except be. There are few responsibilities.

This time is marked by learning, exploration, and a sense of wonder.

It is total dependence during this phase of life.

Life requires nourishment and care.

They willingly follow instructions from parents.

Growth is initially amazingly fast, with obvious achievements.

These primary, formative years are the solid foundation for physical and mental growth.

After a few years, the growth slows down tremendously.

The next years of their life are full of vitality, imagination, playfulness, and passion.

They develop into young people.

There are feelings of love and support from family and friends.

With the introduction of school, they learn, test academic skills, and begin to make comparisons between themselves and others.

They learn social relationships beyond family while interacting with fellow students.

The brain reaches adult size around age seven but continues to develop.

It is slow and steady.

With this being the initial stage of life, it leads to sunrise, where you can start to see things clearer.

These are the developing hours before dawn that are a time of preparation for facing a new day.

There is an awakening and awareness of life's coming attractions.

LIFE OF REB AND DRAN:
06:00 A.M. TO 12:00 P.M. NOON

Reb Begins to Find His Purpose

Reb had grown at a very rapid rate. It was remarkable what one pound at birth could lead to in a year. There was a prominent weight gain because he had been provided many delicious meals. There was a diet of deer, pigs, seals, rodents, fish, salmon, and sweet, dripping honey. The growth was steady, and in one year, Reb had grown to a whopping thirty pounds.

He was happy to have the security of provision from his mom because he knew that the dependency was quickly ending. He would soon be living a self-sufficient life where his only security would be what he had learned from Mom. It was as if time was saying, "Ready or not, here I come."

Though he was a little nervous about the upcoming change, there was something extremely exciting about Reb gaining his independence. The more he observed when he looked around, the more he desired to explore. There were things he could never experience under the roof with his mom. She genuinely feared for his safety.

Reb was a naturally curious bear, and an urgency was deep within him. This propelled him to ask many "why" questions, many of which no one could answer. Even Reb himself did not know how or why the questions kept coming. He just knew he loved getting to the smallest detail, even on what appeared to be the most insignificant matters. He gained satisfaction by figuring things out. It brought things a step closer to understanding the world and life making more sense.

This new season of his life was not as frightening as Reb initially thought it would be. Somehow, he felt very prepared. He had more experience than most with many harrowing adventures and exploits. He had faced several life-or-death situations, and as he said himself, he came out of them quite nicely. He had already seen enough to realize the great vastness of this unique environment. As far as his eyes could see, there were many terrains for him to cover.

Reb's mom was often at a loss as to how she could best help Reb. He was not rebellious, simply curious. She wanted to nourish his independence, but she also needed to keep him safe.

The community bears were often reminded that from the time of Reb's birth, they sensed there was something quite unique about him. One of the prominent things was that he seemed to never slow down. He was climbing, jumping, foraging, and digging constantly. He was a noticeably rambunctious cub.

Though he was given that label, it did not stop Reb. It only confirmed that he was on a mission that others did not understand. Reb accepted it was one of the things that made him so distinct. He held on to the belief that each day would take care of itself and him.

During the many times of exploration, Reb learned about many animals in the forest. He learned that there were some to avoid at all costs. In many cases, it could be a life-or-death decision. However, he had the upper hand on many, because the masses would wisely not challenge a bear. He was large enough to be somewhat of a threat yet small enough to run if that was the best option.

He also learned that other animals looked different, smelled different, ate differently, walked differently, talked differently, and had different survival skills. All this knowledge was very necessary for his survival. He used this information respectfully.

It was great to have all the facts about the other animals, but he also recognized that they did have many things in common. They all ate, slept, thought, and communicated in similar manners. Their bodies and organs were even quite similar (heart, brain, lungs), along with many body systems. The more he learned, the more he realized they are indeed similar. He wondered if other animals thought the way he did. For reasons unknown, he doubted that there were many with mutual thinking.

Living in the forest was like living on a university campus. There were so many things to learn. He wanted to learn them fast so that he would not have to redo these lessons repeatedly. Neither did he want to incur injuries while acquiring knowledge.

One day, Reb heard a ruckus in the woods. He could not tell exactly what it was, but his curiosity would not allow him to sit still. He began to run toward the noise. That was certainly not the typical response from most animals. As he got closer, he realized no other animals were headed that way. Instead, they were running away from the commotion, which in hindsight to him was an incredibly wise choice. He slowed that run to a walking pace and used that time to think about what he was about to encounter. His adventurous nature brought him to the midst of chaos.

As he approached an open field, there were dust clouds so strong it looked like a haboob. It made it difficult to see who or what it was. As he gained his focus, he could see it was an encounter with a cougar and a tiger. His first thoughts were, "Is this the same cougar who was after me at that tree? Was he the one, or was he one of the litters?" He surely was not about to ask! If it was, he hoped the cougar did not recognize him either.

His next thought was, has the cougar lost its mind? Surely the cougar does not stand a chance for a victory. Had he been a betting bear, he would have placed all he had on a tiger victory. Though the tiger was small, it was a totally mismatched confrontation.

As Reb approached the entanglement, he stopped just short of them. Neither the tiger nor the cougar knew if Reb was joining in the fight. While they were trying to figure it all out, the fight stopped.

Suddenly, Reb wondered if they were going to attack him. The tiger looked at Reb with confusion. The cougar looked at Reb with relief. Reb did a quick analysis and, in his mind, realized he was the one in the most danger. They both had the advantage over him. The two of them together could potentially cause him much harm.

His curiosity had brought him to this point, but unfortunately, his life was in a questionable state of survival. He knew his best chances to come out alive were to talk his way out of this situation.

Neither of the animals communicated bear talk very well, so Reb began to cry and use sorrowful facial expressions. Suddenly, Reb screeched very loudly. This certainly got the attention of those two fighting predators. Tears continued to run down Reb's face. It was not often that a tiger and a cougar could witness a bear standing there crying. He used any means necessary to communicate. Reb used vocals and body signals to convey his messages. He was successful in convincing them through his gestures. He charmed them into believing that they were two of the strongest animals in the forest. He stroked their ego, sharing how he admired them from afar. Through previous observations, he had become convinced that they could be instrumental in settling his current dilemma.

He persuaded them to cease fighting and seriously consider joining forces with him to address some common issues that were happening in the forest. He summoned them to the large oak tree by the brook. There, they would meet with some of the other animals and negotiate the surrounding territories. It would no longer be necessary to have these violent confrontations. Those encounters only resulted in bruised and battered bodies and injured egos. If they could focus on the betterment of them all, they would all win.

Reb had not planned this interaction at all. It was a chance meeting that he made the most of, and with his quick thinking, he created a scenario for animal solidarity.

The tiger and the cougar were mesmerized with Reb's suggestion. They wondered, "Who thinks like that?" Because it was so out of the ordinary, they were convinced and agreed to join him. They agreed to help recruit other forest animals to join the meeting. The day quickly arrived, and the attendance was impressive. They were all surprised with how quickly they could all come together on one accord.

He explained to the animals that he had been pondering the social and cultural changes in Gua. He saw humans making major changes to accommodate other humans, yet the animals were losing their natural habitats. Homes and food for the animals were harder to sustain. It was time that they all came together for the betterment of the entire animal kingdom. He solicited their help.

Reb, the cougar, and the tiger all made a compelling case for unity in the forest. They could all work together for a common cause and for the good of all. There was excitement among many of the animals, and a fervent desire was generated.

Against all odds, Reb was successful in convincing the predators. His concerns were ones that the entire animal community shared. It was a miraculous feat to see the forest community come together.

Reb was still curious if it was the same cougar from the previous encounter of when his mom placed him in the tree. He learned that the cougar was new in the forest, so it could not be the same one. Reb was happy about it because he did not want to hinder the progress. Reb was certainly happy to learn that information. He did not want grudges to delay their advances.

Well, word got out that Reb had single-handedly stopped the fight. They reminded themselves that this was the bear that was born in those strange weather conditions, and even then, they knew he was special. It was easier to accept that he was doing this for the entire animal community and not for selfish reasons. The community reasserted the uniqueness of this special bear cub.

Reb gained respect from the other animals, and it was a great confidence booster for him. He felt he had truly made a difference. He always knew he had some special things to do in the world, and this solidified that strong belief.

He began to understand that he would be a strong animal that many would fear. That was never his intention. He genuinely wanted to impact change for himself and others. It was to his advantage to allow his voice to fight his battles. He began to label the new insight as "the power of a roar." A strong roar could send others fleeing for their safety. It could be used for good and bad.

Reb's advice was respected throughout the forest. He was offered increased responsibility. He accepted many of the offers with the honor of being asked. He found himself extremely busy, but that did not bother Reb very much. Most of the things he did were with pleasure.

He was so driven to use every hour to his fullest potential. There were simply not enough hours in a day for Reb, yet he would continue to make the best of the time he was given.

There were many other encounters in the forest. Some were pleasurable, while some were threatening. The commonality of all the experiences was that there were lessons to be learned.

He had an opportunity to show his sincerity once again a few days later.

There had been a severe storm in the forest. Reb was seeking shelter, because the clouds were looking like they might be lingering for a while.

Reb thought that if he could get high enough in a tree on a strong branch, he would be safe until the storm passed. The tree would make a great shelter.

He made it to a strong oak tree, made that climb, and securely wrapped his body around the strongest branch he could find.

He made it just in time before the biggest downpour of rain came crashing down forcefully. And boy, was it hard! To top that, the wind began to blow vigorously. Reb found himself holding on for dear life.

How did he keep getting in these predicaments? he questioned. Why did he find himself once again facing this challenge alone? He did not have the answer to these questions, and he did not have time to figure it out. He just knew he had to make some good decisions quickly to get through this. He aimed to live and see another day.

Through the thick fog from the rain, Reb could barely make out a figure coming toward him.

The rain was blinding, but he could see the figure getting closer. It was a slow crawl, so he could not see the face or full body. His thoughts were, this is someone seeking shelter in the tree, just as he had done. He just hoped it was not a predator to harm him. Finally, he gained enough focus to realize that this was another bear cub.

Now what would he do? Could he find a way to inform the bear cub he was in the tree? Would he climb down and offer his help? Would he ignore the bear? After all, he could put both of their lives at risk.

It only took a split-second decision: he had to help him. He would want someone to help him if he was in a situation like the other bear cub. In fact, he was hoping someone would come along and help them both.

The wind was still overpowering. It had the similar sound of a freight train. Reb had to be loud enough so that the other bear cub could hear him. He began to make a soft wailing sound. He spaced the noise and got a little louder.

Reb could see that the bear cub raised his head and began to look around to see where the sound was coming from.

This was inspiring to Reb. This was an opportunity to help someone. He was more determined than ever to rescue this little bear cub from the storm.

As the bear cub inched his way to the tree in a stupor, Reb began to inch his way down the tree to meet him.

Cautiously, they both began to make the climb. Reb was coming down, and the bear cub was climbing up. At about four tiers in the climb, their eyes met, and though they were still in the storm, they beamed from ear to ear.

Two strangers became instant friends. They could not embrace, because they were still holding on to the tree. It seemed like forever, but they stayed in the same position until the storm began to ease. They were plummeted with rain and wind, but they both knew it was worth it. They did what was necessary to survive.

As Reb was holding on, he thought, "I do not know this bear cub's name, but I will give him the name Storm. This day needs to be commemorated with the assignment of this special name." It would forever remind them of this ordeal.

Finally, the storm passed. They climbed all the way down to the ground. They were finally able to get that anticipated embrace.

And now, an official introduction. The bear cub introduced himself as Cell. Reb heard him, yet he knew he would always refer to his new friend as Storm.

Storm lived in a cave about two miles away. Reb wondered how Storm had gotten so far from home all alone. Storm explained that he had been out foraging with his mom and got separated in the severe weather. The scents had been washed away by the rain. He now just wanted to get back home.

Reb made a promise to Storm to do all he could to help. He needed to get back home himself. It was just a matter of figuring out the best way to make this happen.

Reb's voice seemed trusting and reassuring, so Storm trusted Reb's judgment. He agreed to listen to whatever he was told by Reb. So, he perked up those rounded ears and listened to the stranger who had now become his friend.

Reb's Friendship with Storm

Reb had traveled through the forest many times. He had become familiar with most of the landmarks. He knew the lakes and paths so well, he could travel there without much thought. He knew the straight paths and the crooked paths. He had the quickest routes stored securely in his memory. It was a great skill to have as it helped him tremendously in his maneuvers. He felt confident that with all his recollections, his directions could get Storm back home safely.

The direction Reb gave Storm was perfect. Storm listened, and they both arrived back to their respective dens.

Once they were home safe, they discussed with their families the agony they had experienced. The weather had been scary, but

Reb was prepared to make sound decisions. Reb was especially proud to share his capabilities with his mom. His chest even puffed out a little bigger when he shared his story.

His story was quite convincing. Mom was persuaded that her training had paid off and that Reb knew well the art of survival. She had no reason to worry about Reb's ability to live independently. He had proven his bravery. His sisters were impressed with the harrowing survival story. They admired his strength.

Mom had witnessed the maturity in Reb's life. She had seen many of his life's experiences. In addition, she was certain that there were many other experiences that she had not been privy to know. The adage, "No news is good news," had been prevalent in her life with Reb.

After sharing the story of survival, Reb jumped right in with the story of meeting Storm. He shared how excited he was to encounter his new friend and the circumstances behind their meeting. He had never seen Storm in his area of the woodland before today, but he was glad that they had met. They had made plans to meet up again.

Reb was looking forward to spending time with Storm. They had decided to meet by the same tree on the upcoming Friday at twelve noon. Though it seemed to take forever, Friday finally came.

He knew that he was the older one of the two, but he was not sure about how much. It did not really matter to Reb. He figured they had plenty of time to catch up on minute details. He could show Storm how to avoid some of the pitfalls he had encountered. The things he most looked forward to were having a friend to play with and sharing the explorations of the forest. Since he only had sisters, he would treat him as a little brother.

When Friday came, Reb got up early to complete the chores given to him by Mom. Today's list seemed a little longer than usual. That was probably because he was so anxious to get out of the den. He hurried to get them all done, and off he went. He started with a walk, then a gallop, and finally, he put his running skills to practice. He could now do about 30 mph. He was moving as fast as his short legs could carry him. Though he was running fast, he still had time to think of the fun things they could do and yet remain safe.

He was approaching the last corner in his run, and his heart was racing extremely fast. That was partly because of the run and partly because of the excitement. He started to look for the silhouette he had seen last week while they were in the rain. He knew he would recognize him quickly.

He had arrived at the tree before he knew it, but to his disappointment, he did not see that figure or any other figure standing there. He focused his eyes a second time. Still there was no Storm.

The beaming smile that Reb had all day was suddenly replaced with a disheartening frown. He looked around at all the angels, but he did not see him anywhere. He called his name, but all he

LIVE FAST before your clock strikes 12

heard was an echo. He even climbed up the tree, but he only saw branches and leaves.

In case there was some sort of mix-up, Reb was willing to give him the benefit of doubt. He waited by the tree to see if Storm would show up. Hopefully, he was just running late. He thought of the fact Storm did not know his way around the forest very well. It might take him a while longer. So, he sat down at the base of the tree and waited.

The wait was excruciatingly long. As Reb waited, thoughts began to flood his mind. He wondered if he had the wrong day or time. Was he in the wrong tree? He hoped that nothing had happened to his friend. Reb was so devastated until he began to even question if this had all been a bad dream. With the overwhelming feeling of sadness, Reb waited for six long hours. He was so engrossed during his wait that he forgot he had not eaten since his early morning breakfast.

Tears began to trickle down Reb's face. He knew he could not stay at the tree forever, so with the inescapable verdict, he began to walk back home. It was slow, and each step was heavier than the previous one. It took him twice as long to get home as it did when he came. With a hanging head, he eventually made it back to the den. Walking inside was very difficult. He only had sad news to share.

Mom was so sympathetic to Reb's dilemma. She consoled him the best she could and sat him down for a heart-to-heart talk. She told him about a strong suspicion she had about the reason for the no-show of Storm. She hoped to shine some insight into this current situation.

She remembered hearing from Reb that Storm resided in the southern part of the forest. She was aware of a feud that happened years ago between two bear groups. It was never completely settled, but there was a truce enacted to stop the physical fighting. There was an agreement made to readapt to different environments so they would not have to see one another. Vows had been made to cease all contact and any future relationships. Storm was a part of the southern bear group. For that reason, Mom felt that Storm had been prohibited from meeting with Reb.

This was a total gut punch to Reb. He was devastated. An innocent friendship had now become a fight to overcome a complicated vendetta. Reb's demeanor was unsettling. If the bears could not have a good relationship with one another, what was the hope for peace for other animals and humans?

It suddenly became a bigger issue than the friendship between him and Storm. Maybe there was a greater purpose in their meeting. Reb immediately knew he had to do something to dispel the notion that the two bear groups were doomed to separation.

The next day, Reb used his skills to navigate from his home to the southern part of the forest. He knew where Storm lived because he had given him directions home. For some reason, he was not even nervous. He exuded a confidence that even surprised himself.

LIVE FAST before your clock strikes 12

When he arrived, he saw an open patch of land where some yearling bears were out playing. He approached them as if he had authority to be there. He asked if they knew Cell (Storm) and if so, where did his family reside? They seemed happy to take him to a neighboring den. Cell (Storm), his mom, and two other cubs emerged from the den. Reb and Storm embraced, for they were genuinely happy to see one another.

Storm's mom had already heard of Reb and the meeting in the forest. She had also heard of the bear cub born in those unusual weather conditions. It had been the talk all over the forest. It was still occasionally discussed. She was honored to meet him. She sensed that he was a special bear. She expressed gratitude to Reb for saving her son in the extreme weather. She said that she had never seen him so happy.

Reb shared with Storm's mom why he had given him that name. They both laughed, and she thought it was an appropriate name for her to use with him as a playful nickname.

As they continued to talk, Reb sensed that the feud among the bears was quickly dissipating. Reb remained there for hours, and when he departed, a new resolve had been made. They would no longer carry the previous agreement forward. As of that day, they were committing to new relationships.

Reb went home on cloud nine. He began to share the extended connection with the new bear community. He once again proved that he was certainly a special bear.

He and Storm became friends forever, and their families became friends as well. Their chance meeting reconnected the two bear communities.

Reb's Siblings, His Forever Friends

Grizzly siblings share important roles with one another. They grow up together from babies to capable adults. They interact with one another with genuine heartwarming gestures.

The strong bond is established in their early years. They learn to rely on each other for companionship and safety.

They practice ground skills, survival skills, and social skills among themselves.

These strong traits are some that are often shared with many other animal species.

It is common to see yearlings' grizzly siblings traveling together. Once they are abandoned by their mother, they often stay side by side, eating, sleeping, and denning together.

These attributes are consistent with the life of Reb and his siblings.

Reb grew up in the den cave with three female sister cubs. When they were at home with Mom Sow, they all had individual responsibilities. They would help one another out so they could finish faster. This allowed for more playtime. Some of their best outings were when Mom Sow took them all out together. Though it was a teaching lesson, they were mostly having fun. They learned to fish and hunt, climb trees, and develop strong swimming abilities. They learned to tolerate the very icy water and still swim up to 6 mph. These skills would be beneficial as they would move around in search of salmon and fish.

They did not see him often, but occasionally, they saw their father. They did not spend time with him, but it was a general acknowledgment. This was customary in the life of a bear. The female has the responsibility of raising the cubs, and the male lives in solitude. They were all remarkably close to their mom. They spent most of their time with her unless she was out foraging. She would secure them in a safe place until her return.

This was a regular routine, but then the most unexpected thing happened. Seemingly out of nowhere, Mom kicked them out. They had no choice at all in the matter. There was no explanation, just a new reality for Reb and his siblings. Due to the abruptness of this event, they had to depend on one another. At least there was some familiarity. The siblings all clung tight and started the journey of living without Mom.

Reb considered himself fortunate because he was mostly in charge when they traveled together. He was an excellent protector. Reb's siblings were his best friends, and they felt safe with him.

They spent much of their time playing together. By him being the only boy and bigger in stature, he had to be careful not to hurt them unintentionally. Most of the time, he veered away from physical games with them.

There were opportunities to run, splash, and play. The river was always inviting for a swim, and while they were at it, they could grab a bite to eat from the water. Since they were omnivores, they would change up and grab a big juicy fruit from the nearest fruit tree. Reb and his sisters communicated with body language and voice. Their playfulness helped to develop social attitudes and coordination. They all had great cognitive abilities. They would learn things from each other and the other bears around the forest. They would wag their head from side to side to indicate they were ready to play. It was important to communicate with each other, because everyone was not in a playful mood at the same time.

Most of the day, the time was spent eating. It took an enormous amount of food per day to feed them all. As they grew, they were like eating machines. They did not all like the same thing, but they all liked to eat. Because of the great training from their mom and their keen sense of remembering, they knew where to find food.

They were extremely close to one another, but the day came when Reb had to venture from them and become independent. They had become so dependent on Reb and his many skills that they doubted their ability to survive on their own. Reb assured them that he would keep a watchful eye on them, and he stressed his confidence in their abilities.

They adjusted to daily life without Reb, and as he had predicted, they were okay out on their own.

They remembered the day of separation from their mom. The separation from Reb was not as traumatic, but it did rekindle memories and feelings that brought them to tears. Their consolation was that they had each other. It was reassuring to know so much about foraging, as they had learned from their mom and Reb. They accepted that there would be other family separations as they started their own lives, creating their individual families.

They were extremely proud of Reb, and they had watched the attention he was getting from all the animals. They heard the rumors throughout the forest that he was doing exceptional things to help make Gua an even better place for them all.

They stayed together, eating, sleeping, and denning. They became so sufficient that they allowed some of the other female cubs to join, forming a sleuth in their hunts.

With the construction of new houses around the forest, food was beginning to be scarcer. They did not have as many choices for foraging. It took them longer on their hunting expeditions. Of course, some of their fun times were cut short.

Reb heard of the current dilemma, and even though he was not close by, he would find ways to do them as he did his mom. He would leave scraps at their den whenever he could.

They had the opportunity to see Reb one day, and they were ecstatic. They were hoping for a chance to reunite with him. They pledged to help him on his missions when he needed them but would stay out of his way when that was the best thing to do. He wished that that could happen, but he respectfully declined their offer. He assured them that he would continue to do what he could to protect the forest for not just his family, but all the animals. Many of the animals were vulnerable to predators, and he would be helping them as well.

Most realized that it was too dangerous to challenge a bear, therefore, most of them were little threat to the bear community.

The biggest challenge was the humans who chose to do recreational hunting, often destroying bear families. They attempted to avoid humans as much as they could. That was why humans seldom saw them in the wild. With their keen senses and their ability to move silently, they could hide inconspicuously. He stressed the importance of the work he was doing, and he anticipated impressive results.

Reb's sisters were even more proud of him and shared good wishes as they departed a second time.

It was now the summer months, and this was the mating season. Reb's sisters were being courted by the boar bears, and they were also ready to start a family. They began to look for a home range to prepare for cubs. They settled in areas near their mom sow. They would not be together but would be in close proximity to one another.

When the winter came, Reb's sisters were all having cubs. They knew the routine of birthing and accepted the role of motherhood with immense joy. Reb was not there, but he heard of the births, and he could not be a prouder uncle three times.

Dran's School Friend, Boss

Dran had seen and done astonishing things in his young years. It was hard to believe that Dran was approaching his teenage years. Time had moved along amazingly fast. He found himself walking down the halls of middle school. He contemplated these innovative studies at school because he was well prepared academically for the challenge. He had continued to exceed the cognitive expectations from educators. They often relied on Dran to assist with their efforts in explaining lessons to other students. Sometimes, as a fellow peer, Dran was more relatable to his fellow classmates.

The likelihood of new friendships and experiences was also intriguing to him. He had many benefits to gain at this junction of his life. There were people, places, and things that were in place to enhance these wonder years. He had many people cheering him on to greater levels. He maintained a stellar reputation within the community. He was still inquisitive yet incredibly involved with whatever was going on in the community. There were always things to do, so he had little idle time. There was his usual routine as well as extracurricular activities.

In school, he would often finish his work ahead of all his classmates. He would then just sit there quite bored. This became extremely frustrating to him as well as to his teachers. His teachers tried many options that would keep down the distractions. The aim was to keep him occupied. However, neither the options nor the teachers were successful.

The teacher tried bringing extra work to keep him busy. They did not want him to continue to be a distraction to the other students. That strategy did not work either, because Dran would finish that work accurately and amazingly fast.

As options ran out, his teacher, the principal, and Dran's parents met to discuss a course of action to best address Dran's needs. Sometimes they would work, but unfortunately, the suggestions were usually short-lived, and Dran continued to show that the schoolwork was of little challenge.

Two grades later, Dran met the person who would eventually become his favorite teacher. She was in awe of Dran's ability, and she soon recommended him for the accelerated school program outside of their regular classroom. It required traveling to a different campus for expanded studies. The school provided the necessary transportation. Her academic evaluation had placed him, at minimum, three grade levels above his fellow students. The special program was where Dran excelled. He not only surpassed his basic classes, but he also discovered other hidden talents as well.

He expressed a very natural ability in arts and performance. There were few things that made him happier than expressing himself onstage. He had the uncanny ability to create a variety of characters and playmates in his head. His creativity developed to the point that he was able to do several characters simultaneously in a freestyle manner. He had no problem capturing a craving audience. He would often highlight this talent without any previous preparation for a spontaneous performance. each of them. Many doors of opportunity began to open for Dran. He was given many platforms to perform his amazing talents.

Dran's parents were his biggest supporters. They consented for him to attend several advanced studies that proved to be exceptionally beneficial. There, he learned new techniques and skills that he could incorporate in his performances. He continued to practice them as often as possible. Dran had shown great maturity and an eagerness to learn and excel.

In addition to academics and performing arts, he was involved in several other activities. Dran loved music and writing and even tried his hand at preparing gourmet meals. He enjoyed expanding his knowledge in a variety of areas. He constantly added more to his agenda. He played instruments and once started a duo group called Twice as Nice. Their duration as a group was short-lived, but they recorded an original song.

During these years of honing his many talents, he met some of his closest friends. They shared similar interests and moral values, and most of all, they cherished the joy of having fun. These friendships were precious to Dran. The experiences they shared sealed a close bond that they knew would last a lifetime and even beyond.

With Dran's magnetic personality, he usually had a group around him. He was considered the life of the party whenever

LIVE FAST before your clock strikes 12

he came around. His upbeat demeanor was a usual good fix for anyone feeling down.

People would observe how busy he was, but they noticed he always had time for others. Dran consistently found ways to include others in his circle. He had a particular interest in anyone who was alone most of the time. Somehow, they stuck out to him like a sore thumb. He would turn on his charm and make them feel special. They would leave feeling he was their best friend.

When he would greet a person or depart from a person, he would offer the biggest hugs. Soon, others referred to them as his "Bear Hugs." These gestures always produced big, joyful expressions of laughter and smiles. Dran had accomplished what he wanted when he helped someone to smile.

He was always a voice of reason. When faced with questionable decisions among friends, he attempted to use his gift of persuasion to yield to the least of the available evils.

At school, he noticed one of the students, who spent most of his time alone. At lunch, he would even go outside and sit on one of the benches. Dran had even observed him taking a nap while other students ate lunch. In the hallways, he would speak, but he was never in prolonged conversation with anyone. These things were concerning to Dran.

In keeping with his natural intuition, he walked outside and sat on the bench during lunch. He asked the student if it was okay to sit with him. The reply was soft-spoken, but he answered,

"Sure." They exchanged introductions and then began to talk about the classes they shared together.

He shared that his name was Bedford Oden SaddleSen. The length of his name had caused people to develop something shorter. People always called him Boss. It certainly was much easier to pronounce.

Dran noticed he was not eating anything, so he offered him a bag of chips that he falsely claimed he did not want. Surprisingly, Boss accepted the bag and gobbled it down quickly. They talked until the bell rang. Lunch was over, but they agreed to talk again.

This arrangement continued for the remainder of the school week. Each day, Dran would share his lunch with his new friend, who gladly accepted it.

Eventually, Dran encouraged Boss to come inside for lunch, where he introduced him to some of the other students. This was so encouraging to Boss, and he began to consider Dran a devoted friend.

As Boss became more comfortable with Dran, he began to share some of his family situations.

One of the more secretive things was that his father lost his job, and the family was facing severe financial hardship. Dran knew that there was an issue, since Boss never had lunch or money to purchase food. He was glad he waited to allow Boss to share on his own terms. Dran could not do much financially, but he produced a way to help his friend without drawing attention. He had considered it an honor that Boss would trust him with something so sensitive.

The next morning, Dran asked his mother to make his lunch a little healthier because he often was hungry before the school day was done. Mom realized Dran had had a growth spurt and could need more food after being busy at school all day. She did not question his request for extra because he was even eating more at home during the dinner meals.

He secretly took a separate bag, and when he arrived at school, he divided the lunch into two parts. He handed it off to Boss before their first class together. When lunchtime came, Boss joined the students in the lunchroom. Sometimes he ate with Dran, but on other days, he ate lunch with some of his other new friends. This arrangement brought satisfaction to each of them.

Each morning, Mom packed the healthy lunch for Dran. Each day, he came home with an empty lunch box. There were days Mom would give him a few dollars in case he wanted to purchase even more at school to eat.

Boss was incredibly grateful for the lunch every day, but he had begun to feel guilty that Dran was bringing enormous amounts of food from home.

This went on for a few weeks. Dran was wondering what else he could do. This was working, but it was not a long-term solution.

Dran's father had informed him that the weekend was going to be beautiful weather and it would be an ideal time to go fishing.

If he would like, he could even invite a friend to join them for this adventure. It sounded like a wonderful idea to Dran, and he immediately thought of his new friend Boss. The arrangements were made, and Boss came home with him on Friday from school. He would stay over and go fishing with him and his father on Saturday morning. They would take him home on Saturday afternoon. Boss was so excited. He had never fished before, and it gave him something to look forward to. Dran's dad would show them both their best strategies for bringing in a good catch.

While the guys planned fishing, Mom and the girls planned a day of shopping.

On Friday night, for dinner, Mom fixed spaghetti and meatballs. The family loved this dish, but Mom noticed Dran did not eat much. Boss, however, enjoyed it so much that he asked for seconds. Mom quickly obliged. He devoured it quickly. Mom got the impression that Boss wanted more but was embarrassed to ask. Before she could offer more, Dran spoke up and said, "Boss, save room for dessert." Mom had prepared apple pie. It was one of the family's favorites, even more so because the apples grew in their backyard. Talk about a homegrown product; it couldn't be any closer! They all enjoyed the special dish. Boss extended the compliment by declaring, "The food is delicious. I really enjoyed it."

After dinner, Dran and Boss went to the bedroom. They laughed and talked and planned for the next day. They got a chance to play a video game before preparing for bed. This was such a fun night for Boss, and he could not wait till Saturday.

The parents were not trying to, but they overheard Boss discussing his family situation with Dran. Boss shared that at the end of the school year in two months, they would move in to live with his grandparents. He would no longer be a student at their middle school. He was just beginning to enjoy it there, but his family could no longer afford to stay in their home.

This saddened Dran's parents very much to hear this. It explained the reason Dran took extra food to school. In typical Dran style, he was showing compassion. By the next day on the fishing trip, things slowly unfolded. Boss began to open up to Dran's father. The boys even told the truth about the extra lunches. Dran's father never shared that they heard the conversation the night before.

Dad was not upset with Dran, but he shared that they were children handling adult issues. There might be something he could do to help once he was able to find out Boss's dad's work qualifications.

He complimented Dran on being a true confidential friend to Boss. He emphasized how amazing and mature he was and made him immensely proud to be his dad. They moved on with their discussion and focused on the fun at the lake.

Dran's father taught them the art of fishing. They had a great catch of twelve fish. They had a variety of types and sizes.

Fishing was going well for the three of them. Dran was curious as to whether he could do this alone. He walked down the shore with his fishing equipment to practice what he had just learned. He left Boss with his dad so that they could continue to talk.

Dran had remarkable results. He brought in a catch of fifteen fish with minimal effort. It was as if someone left them close by just for him. Where did all those fish come from so quickly? He did not make much attempt at all, and the fish were there waiting. He did not have an explanation, so he would just enjoy the catch.

Dran ran back to his dad and Boss to show them his bucket of fish. It was unbelievable that he could catch that many fish so quickly. Dran only said to his dad that he was an excellent teacher.

Later that day, Dran and his father took Boss home. He asked if he could talk to Boss's parents. That was not a problem for Boss. He was happy for them to meet. When they arrived, they handed over the twelve fish they had caught to Boss to share with his family.

Dran's father shared information that could be helpful in Boss's father finding new employment. He had no guarantees but encouraged him to follow up on the job lead he gave him.

Dran and his father left there feeling they had made a difference in Boss's family life.

Dran went home still wondering where those fish really came from. He knew he did not really catch them.

Within the next month, Boss's father had secured a new job at the company Dran's father recommended. They were able to stay in their home, and Boss remained at school. The two families had opportunities to share time with one another, and they became lasting friends.

Dran's Siblings, His Eternal Friends and Confidants

Dran's siblings were his best friends. They often spoke among themselves of how blessed they were to be a part of such a dynamic and loving family. Regardless of what was going on, he could count on them to be in his corner.

In later years, he understood it would be extremely hard to maneuver through life without them. He realized that he gained a wealth of knowledge from them that could never be taught at any university. He would like to believe they learned a thing or two from him as well. They synchronized and complemented one another extremely well.

They bonded over their shared history, the same environment, shared memories, shared experiences, and of course, shared parents. They could even share secrets and know that they were trusted confidants.

He would sometimes have disagreements with them, but he soon learned it was often better to let them win. He learned that winning the battle does not always win the war. He usually found a way to get whatever he wanted regardless of who took the winning title. Being the older brother did have its benefits.

They were never concerned about these spats, for they were never long-lasting. This was only a result of each of their strong wills.

Of course, they were different, but none of the differences outweighed their commitment to their loving family.

LIVE FAST before your clock strikes 12

They had a lifelong unconditional love for one another. They looked after the others' best interests, and they stayed in a protective mode when it came to outside interference. There was a strong emotional connection with tolerance and patience. Their sibling bond was undeniable. They would cheerfully share with one another, whether it was food, money, things, or advice.

They were the greatest at making each other laugh. There was seldom any sadness, just fun and laughter. The household was always loud and joyful. They particularly loved board games. The winner would always rub it in within their sibling group.

They loved to sing and perform together and even referred to themselves as New BDBT Group, taking initials from their name. Each of them would take turns as lead singer, and they would all write lyrics. Soon they were playing instruments and creating incredible sounds. There were some remarkably good shows for their family and friends.

There were a few times they had to cover for one another so none of them would be in trouble with the parents.

Dran was driving a car at sixteen. He had the responsibility of getting his sister to school on time each morning and both returning after school with no detours. There were to be no additional riders in the car.

During the first few weeks of school, things flowed well with the driving arrangements. But then, the parents became aware that other students were getting rides from Dran back to their homes.

His sisters failed to mention the riders to their parents. They could not bear to see Dran get in trouble, especially because of them. For some reason, Dran felt he was innocent of wrongdoing because he did not think the rules applied to his friends. It was typical Dran. He was always trying to help someone.

The sincerity of Dran was reason enough for Dran's parents to issue only a warning for this act of disobedience. However, it did come with a stern warning. From that day forward, they did not hear of additional riders, but they wouldn't say it never happened.

It was during the Christmas holiday season when Dran's parents decided to enter a float in the Christmas parade. It would display the veterinarian business sign owned by Dran's father.

They all worked extremely hard to ensure it would be a beautiful display. In addition to these efforts, they would have some live animals riding on the float. There would be a sheep, a pig, a llama, a goat, a cow, and a turkey.

They were securely placed on the float, anchored and fenced for extra protection.

They knew that the animals would be a pleasant surprise for the families in attendance.

On the day of the parade, the streets were lined with a huge crowd. People had traveled from other cities to witness the much-anticipated festivities.

Dran was the designated person to throw out the candy to the children who patiently waited on the streets.

As the band began to play, it startled some of the animals. Their float was too close for comfort. They began to get restless as they were confined on the float.

The siblings tried to calm the animals down, but they were increasingly agitated.

The parade line moved slowly through the street, and the screams and cheers were heard loudly throughout the crowd. The children especially loved seeing wild animals, and they attempted to get close to touch them. No one was prepared for what came next.

With a totally unexpected gesture, the animals broke the anchor and the fence and disconnected from their security. They jumped off the float into the crowd of people. The screams got louder from all the parade attendees. Dran and his sisters tried to gather the loose animals. He even tried to give them the candy that was designated for the children. The animals didn't want candy, they wanted freedom.

Dran's father was the driver and did not notice for a while what all the commotion was about. As soon as there was a clear space, he exited from the parade and immediately joined in gathering the animals.

The parade temporarily halted until all the animals were secure. They were carried back to their safe and comfortable environment.

There was lots of conversation from the community about this unpleasant experience. The siblings put the blame on each other, but eventually, they all took responsibility for the role they played in the Christmas parade disaster.

It later became a recurring story that brought laughs to the siblings repeatedly. Each time the story was told, they would embellish the details until eventually, it became a folktale.

Their many experiences solidified the lasting love they continued to share with one another.

The sibling had established such a strong bond that it was difficult to see Dran graduate from high school and leave home. It was equally difficult for Dran.

They were not ready, but in their hearts, they knew he was. home, the siblings were not ready. They knew they would miss the daily interaction of Dran. However, they were so proud of him, and they knew he would do extremely well with whatever path he took in his life. He had a portion of the world to conquer.

They never doubted they could call him anytime. He would do what he always did. He would help with whatever he could to make their lives easier.

They always had the assurance of his love and support whenever and wherever he was.

Dran's Acceptance Letter

School had been even more than Dran hoped for. He was doing extremely well academically, and he had excelled in his extracurricular and fine arts endeavors. His friendships were rewarding, and he and his family enjoyed one another tremendously.

He was completing his high school and was excited about his upcoming college career. He would be approximately two hours from home, which was perfectly fine with him, but in the meantime, he had an opportunity for a once-in-a-lifetime training.

The school year was ending, and summer vacation was close in sight. This summer brought with it a wonderful opportunity to attend a prestigious university. They were offering an eight-week summer internship with studies in the seven areas of discipline of fine arts. There would be a study of painting, sculpture, architecture, poetry, music, literature, and dance. This was exciting, because Dran had an interest in all these areas of study. It was an unbelievable opportunity to have these offered under the same roof. This would be a dream come true for Dran. What better way to spend summer vacation than doing something so intense that you really loved? Dran was aware of a couple of students from his school who had also applied to participate in the same program. He thought about how great it would be for several people from the same area to be there together.

He assured his parents that if he were rewarded with the opportunity to attend, he would be on his best behavior. He would also take advantage of learning as much as he could.

His parents were excited for Dran and this rare opportunity. Without hesitation, they agreed to his attending, provided he continued to do well in school. They filled out all the necessary paperwork and mailed it to the university on time to meet the deadlines. They realized there were many other students across the country vying for the limited slots. The university's final decision would be contingent on end-of-the-school-year grades. There was limited space, so only the top students would be chosen.

Dran felt good that all pertinent items had been submitted and details properly addressed to complete the preparation process. Now it was a matter of practicing patience while waiting for the favorable reply.

In about three weeks, the response from the university came in the mail. When Dran got in from school, he noticed the letter lying on the top of a mail stack on the coffee table. Mom had placed it unopened there so it would be difficult for Dran to miss seeing it.

Dran decided to wait until after dinner before he opened the letter. He did not want to risk losing his appetite if it was a negative response. After each bite, he thought of what was in that envelope. He agonized over whether it would be a yes or no answer. He was anxious and a little afraid of what the letter would read. Dran knew he had the support of his parents and sisters regardless of the response from the university. However, he sure hoped the answer would be favorable.

LIVE FAST before your clock strikes 12

Dinner was finally finished. Dran got up from the table, grabbed the letter, and walked slowly to the chair. They all gathered around him.

He did not want the mystery and agony to continue, so he quickly ripped the letter open. He unfolded the letter and began to read. "We are pleased to inform you that you have been selected as a participant in our summer intern program."

There were other details that included dates, times, supplies, and directions, but Dran did not want to focus on those minor details. There would be time for that later. Right now, he wanted to bask in the excitement. He jumped up and down and bellied out a big scream. The excitement was contagious, so they all joined hands and jumped up and down with Dran.

This would be a summer to remember. He would meet new friends and learn so many new things about studies he loved.

There were some concerns and trivial details to consider, but it all could wait. There was still a little time to figure it out, and they did not want to dampen Dran's excitement.

Right now, it was time to celebrate, and celebrate they did! There was pizza and ice cream. These were two of Dran's favorite things to eat. He certainly ate more than he should have.

Later that evening, they finished reviewing the acceptance letter. They compiled a list of the things Dran needed to carry with him. They decided what he already had and what his parents needed to purchase.

At the top of the list was his friend Benno. He felt a little embarrassed to carry a stuffed animal to a university campus, but there was no way he was going to leave him in Gua. This time, he would watch every move he made and never allow him to be out of his sight.

On his list were pictures of his sisters. He knew he would miss them so much, and he could not take them with him, but he could see them every day.

Dran wanted to decorate his room with a wild forest theme. He thought it would remind him of Gua without making him too homesick. He just loved the vibes of the forest. The school colors were orange and green. Therefore, his room would include these colors. Their school mascot was a giant grizzly bear dressed in an orange and green T-shirt. He could not wait to get one of those shirts for Benno. Besides the academic portion, Dran thought the bear was the thing that most attracted him to the university. He loved that mascot!

When Dran went back to school the following Monday, he was allowed to take his acceptance letter. He proudly showed his teacher and his friends. They were happy for Dran and wished him the best. None of them were surprised at his achievements. They felt that this was the beginning of many other opportunities. He was saddened to hear that the other two students that applied did not receive an acceptance letter. Dran would miss them, but he would share the things he learned when he returned.

LIVE FAST before your clock strikes 12

It was countdown time again. He had exactly twelve weeks (about three months) before he would leave for his summer trip. He remembered Mom had made a countdown calendar for him in elementary school for the school field trip to the animal reservation. This time, he would make one for himself.

He found two sheets of construction paper that were orange and green. He also had some bear stickers remaining from the souvenir shop at the reservation. He designed a calendar to place on the refrigerator. Each day, he placed a bear sticker on the day's date. This helped him realize the trip was really happening. It was not a dream.

His friends and family talked about it consistently with him. Some days, Dran thought that they sounded as if they were the ones going on the summer trip. He was happy, though, that so many were excited for him. He could not wait for the adventure to begin. Over the next weeks, much of the preparation was done for Dran's big trip.

Dran continued to mark down the dates on his calendar. The calendar got a little smudged and a little dirty, but Dran was faithful to mark it each day.

When the calendar reached two weeks out, Dran's parents helped him begin the packing. He had luggage and boxes.

The distance was further than his parents wanted to drive, so Dran and his parents were flying to the university destination.

This would be Dran's first airline flight, so he was thrilled that both his parents were accompanying him.

The parents were thrilled that they would have a chance to see Dran's temporary residents and meet the people in charge of the program.

The day came when Dran put the final sticker on his calendar. The next day was the actual flight. Dran's parents had arranged a taxi to pick them up and drive them to the airport.

Dran was so excited. His stomach was doing somersaults. When the taxi arrived and they were all seated inside, they all introduced themselves.

The taxi driver went first. "Good morning, my name is Mr. Bear." They all laughed at that unusual name. Mr. Bear had a great deal of facial hair. His head of hair was shaggy. His beady eyes were close together, peeping through his excessive hair on his face. Mr. Bear explained that his actual name was Bearon, but everyone called him Bear for short. "You all are my first passengers today," he said. The more they looked at him, the more they understood why he had that name.

Then they introduced themselves. It was Dran's opportunity to share all about his summer trip to the university, and of course, he told him about Benno. He shared that this was his first flight, and he also admitted that he was nervous.

Mr. Bear was very reassuring, especially to Dran. He said he was proud of his acceptance to the prestigious university and

LIVE FAST before your clock strikes 12

knew he would do well. He talked to Dran as if they had known each other a long time, even though they had just met. There was something calming about Mr. Bear's demeanor.

He told Dran to just remember why he was traveling, take deep breaths, and find ways to distract his mind by refocusing. He even suggested that he make sure Benno is okay on the flight by keeping a conversation with him. He helped to calm Dran's fear, and when they arrived at the airport, he felt so much better.

Mr. Bear helped with the luggage, and they said their goodbyes. When Dran turned to leave, Mr. Bear bent down and made direct eye contact with Dran. His lips moved slightly between the dense surrounding hair on his face. He spoke in a soft voice, saying, "Dran, I'll see you a little later." As Mr. Bear reached out his glove-covered hand, Dran could see hair protruding around the outer borders of his hand. He really was hairy.

Dran was now excited instead of fearful. He reminded himself of the flight tips Mr. Bear had shared with him. It worked. The flight was comfortable and turbulence-free for Dran and his parents. It was perfect for him. On his way from the plane, he met the pilot and was given a first flight pin for his bravery.

It was now the time they had all been waiting for. It was time to get to the university. Dran's parents arranged a taxi to take them there. Soon, the taxi rode up to the loading airport lane, and the driver got out to greet them. As he shook his glove-covered hairy hand, he introduced himself. "Hi, my name is Mr. Oso."

It would take months for Dran to learn that the name was the Spanish name for Bear.

He loaded the taxi, and they headed to the university. Dran's newest adventure had begun.

Encounter at the Outdoor Theater

Dran's eight weeks (about two months) at the university were phenomenal. It had been a memorable summer experience. The skills he acquired and often mastered were a great confidence booster. He was optimistic that all the many new skills would open the doors for greater opportunities. He delighted in the assurance that he had grown in a variety of ways to include standing taller. He was sure he had grown at least three inches.

There were life-changing experiences during the many weeks of being there. He was convinced he had matured during his time from home. There had been many opportunities to make independent decisions. He thought he handled them extremely well. At least, there were no negative consequences. There was no doubt in his mind that his family would be so proud of him and all that he had achieved.

LIVE FAST before your clock strikes 12

The students would all be returning home in a couple of days. Dran's parents would not be traveling with him on the return trip, but he was okay to travel alone. He did have the school shuttle bus to get him to the airport.   This was only his second airline trip. His parents would meet him at Gua airport at the designated time, which also was reassuring.

He would miss his time at the university, but he looked forward to seeing his family and friends. He was sure they missed him too.

There had been many things there that reminded him of Gua. The mountains and the forest were the two things that reminded him the most. While he walked around, he sometimes forgot he was sixteen hours from home. There were striking similarities. He would, however, remember the distinct traits that made some areas of the environment quite unique. The university itself was one of the greatest differences.

There was a grand finale performance scheduled on the night before the camp was concluded. Dran had practiced very diligently for his cherished starring role at this climax performance. He wished Mom and Dad could be there to see his performance, but he understood that it was too far to drive for one day. He was happy to find out that the performance was being recorded and would be available for purchase soon. His family would be able to see the show after all. This gave Dran an even greater incentive to do his absolute best. He had rehearsed his lines as often as he could. At night, he would sit outside with Benno in front of him. He allowed him to listen to him practice and watch all his performing gestures. He knew Benno could not respond to praise or criticize him, but he loved having a captured audience.

The day of the performance had beautiful weather. It was not as hot as it had been, which was a welcome climate for their outdoor show. The excessive heat would sometimes cause the makeup to melt. Between the costumes and lighting, the stage could be sweltering. They were grateful that they did not have that as a concern that evening. The tall trees gave the perfect breeze to keep them comfortable.

There was a beautiful outdoor theater with the natural backdrop of the sloping mountains.

You could even see the snowcaps at the mountain's peak. Dran always thought it was strange to see snow on the top when it could be extremely hot on the ground. It was further enhanced by the stars twinkling in the clear blue skies. It was a marvelous stage to display their talents as the finale before leaving the area.

The cast took their places and waited for the next instructions. They were shaking off their jitters as they stood by. It was the perfect time to initiate some of the things they had learned over these many weeks.

They began some deep breathing and stretching exercises. There were a few minutes to review a few lines and hope that they were recalled at the appropriate time. Lastly, they had water to hydrate, but not too much. Bathroom breaks were not practical during performances.

"Lights, camera, and action," the director shouted through his megaphone. This was it! The performance began.

Dran was first on stage. His opening lines were, "I can see so much beauty in these beautiful, picturesque islands of the sky."

He then raised his arms, looked up, and in a deep act of reverence, he uttered the word, "Awe"!

The audience responded just as they had hoped. They looked up toward the sky following Dran's lead and gave out in unison that same loud word, "Awe"! Those sounds from the audience vibrated through the summit. This was a great and powerful opening to their performance. These mountains seemed to bring out the spirit of voyager in their spectators. They seemed conscientious and yet territorial when it came to their majestic peaks. Many considered the mountains as a symbol of stability and strength. The familiar environment for the audience was the perfect place for a summer night entertainment outing.

The performance went well from start to finish without any hitches. Dran gave a stellar performance and hated it to end. The audience was captivated by the thrilling performance of the cast. They had responded to each scene appropriately throughout the show. Afterward, there were several standing ovations.

The director and all the cast were elated. The show was a home run. In theater terms, they experienced the theater sentiment, "Break a leg."

Now that the performance was over, it was bittersweet. It was only a one-night show. The performers wished they had another show, and the audience seemed to wish the same.

Gratitude for the experience was what they all reiterated. They hugged and gave each other high fives. Some even dropped a few tears from their eyes. There were also phone number and address exchanges with the hope of staying in touch. They gave their in-

LIVE FAST before your clock strikes 12

structors a deserving standing ovation too. They had practiced much patience with them while sharing their love of teaching.

By now, they were ready to devour some food. They had not eaten in about four hours, so they all had a sizable appetite. Dran scheduled to meet his friends at the dining facility. The sooner he got dressed, the sooner he could eat and say their goodbyes.

Dran hurried to the dressing room to change from the heavy costumes to his regular clothes.

He took off the heavy jacket first and draped it across the top of the door. It did not take long at all to change his clothes.

Once he changed, he began to gather up the complete costume to return to the design studio. He reached to grab the jacket, but it was not there. He opened the door and looked to see if it had fallen to the ground. The jacket was gone!

In a state of panic, he ran around asking if someone took his jacket by mistake. That seemed unlikely because no one else had the same jacket. He had only stood in the same spot in the dressing room. There was a mystery as to where the jacket could be. He felt better asking though, just to rule out any unintentional mistakes. He went back to the dressing room to retrace his steps and try and figure out what happened.

Dran could not eat until he found it, so he continued to search. He could not believe that on his last night, there was trouble. Things had been perfect up until this time.

Dran suddenly heard screams and feet stomping and running toward him. Some of the cast members were headed toward the dressing room. When Dran saw them, he saw fright all over their faces. "Stay inside!" they yelled. Several cast members came bursting into the room.

They began to tell Dran about what happened after they ate. They were heading back to their rooms to finish packing. There was a shortcut that they had previously used. It seemed like a safe way to speed up the process. To their surprise, about half of the way back, they stumbled into a group of yearling bears in the woods.

Immediately, Dran wondered if those bears had his jacket. If so, he was not going to allow the bears to prevent his eating or jeopardize him leaving to go home. He had all the motivation he needed to find that jacket. If the bears had it, he would surely find it.

Without delay, he stomped out of the room and headed toward the forest. Dran had hardly reached the entry to the woods when he spotted the three yearling bears pulling on something on the ground. He initially thought it could be a person but soon realized it was a piece of clothing. As he got closer, he observed it was his jacket. They were using it as a toy or checking to see if food was in the pockets.

He kept walking toward them at a steady pace. He did not put any thought into it. He was on a mission to retrieve something that belonged to him before it was destroyed.

In an instant, the yearlings stopped and stared at him. Dran knew not to stare back at them, as they would perceive it as a challenge. He turned his head quickly to break his glare.

Without warning, two of the yearlings ran away. They returned to the woods they came from.

The third yearling picked up the jacket with his mouth. He began to walk toward Dran. When he reached a proximity near him, he stopped again and stared at Dran. He had a good look into the yearling's eyes. They were small round sized with no pupils. They were set close to the ground, widely spaced, and forward-facing. The night light reflected a red tint in the deep brown eyes. He never dreamed he would be that close to a grizzly.

The next move was unimaginable. The yearling shook his head from side to side and pivoted to walk toward the dressing room. Dran followed close behind him. When they reached the front of the door, the yearling dropped the jacket. He turned toward Dran and winked his eyes. During this time, Dran started to shake all over. He had not been frightened until now.

As the yearling started his walk back toward the woods, he turned and gave another glance to Dran. This time, it was with a smile. The yearling bear stopped and looked at Dran for a few seconds. During that encounter, calmness came over Dran. The yearling bear then turned and ran away as fast as he could.

Dran grabbed the jacket, and he ran just as fast as the bear to share this unbelievable experience with the others.

He returned the undamaged jacket to the studio and was constantly babbling about all the details. He could not get his words out fast enough.

Dran was not sleepy or hungry anymore. He went to his room reflecting on all that had happened. He slept very lightly, because he was very anxious to get home and share with everyone the escapade he experienced.

This was a haunting adventure and an enthralling climax from the summer program. For the rest of his life, he would never forget and share the story of that bear!

It's 12:00 Noon

Who knew in the world,
I had so many things to explore.
When one way closes,
there's always another door.
They learned to push them open,
often without a knock,
but they had to do it fast, you see,
for it's already twelve o'clock.

LIVE FAST before your clock strikes 12

A Time to Bloom and Achieve:
ATTRIBUTES AT 06:01 TO 12:00 P.M.

There is a transition from childhood to adulthood.
Name labels of adolescents, teenagers, and
young adults are interchangeable.
Life is full of mostly fun, food, and good health.
Hormones are often raging, adjusted to puberty and young adult status.
Mental adjustments are consistently being made.
The invincible attitude is often prevalent.
There is a concerted effort to establish the future.
This is mostly done by getting an education, learning skills and crafts,
making friends, looking for partners, starting to build a career.
The focus to figure out one's purpose in life becomes a priority.
Goals are pursued with vigor.
Relationships deepen, and career paths
may become more defined.
Professional and personal achievements are stabilized.
There are decisions made about financial earning possibilities.
There are pressures of maintaining success.
Attempts are made to balance personal life and career aspirations.
This can also be a time of loneliness, confusion, and fear about what steps to take next.

VIVIAN WARD NEWTON

This is the time for harnessing one's strengths and fostering emotional intelligence.

LIFE OF REB AND DRAN:
12:00 P.M. NOON TO 6:00 P.M.

Reb Against All Odds: The Big Protest

Reb had been away from his family for many years. He still missed everyday contact, but occasionally, he would run into his parents or siblings in the forest. He was now an uncle several times over, and he would even see his nieces and nephew cubs playing out in the homelands.

He often reflected on how far he had come from being such a small cub himself, but now he weighed in at over four hundred pounds. He was close to being the weight of a full-grown grizzly bear. If he kept eating those big meals, he would be double that weight soon.

Being an omnivore did allow his diet to have great variation. He could rotate between consuming prey or plants. It was usually based on his location. Whatever was convenient mostly worked for his palate.

Reb was having remarkable success in his ability to hunt for larger prey. He served as a mentor to many of the younger bears. He taught them the most efficient skills for hunting. It was an enjoyable day when they could hunt together, relax, and then share a scrumptious meal. Seeing them hunt independently was an even more rewarding day.

When Reb saw the cubs playing around the woodlands, he was compelled to think about his own legacy. He, along with others, recognized he had become more mature and responsible. Establishing his own family had now become a nagging desire for him. He had seen the perky ears of the sows out in the woodlands, which was an added incentive to begin his family.

He thought about it often, but he would repeatedly conclude that now was an unsuitable time to start his own family. There were too many distractions and uncertainties in the forest. Until there was more stability in his surroundings, Reb opted to wait until he felt secure enough to handle the extra responsibility.

The forest was constantly being altered by land developments implemented by humans. There had been defined animal boundaries established for centuries. Everything and everybody knew their safe areas.

Then there were areas that were sought after and marked as secure areas for individual animal families. Many animals would go to great lengths to find the perfect home for themselves and their offsprings. The search often took months to complete.

Once it was established, it was usually respected by any opposing animal that had an interest in the same space. They could easily evaluate by the marking if it were to their advantage to provoke any opposition.

This was a practice widely accepted throughout the forest. It was often easier and wiser to accept the inevitable than to risk the consequences of a fight. It was a respectable sign of wisdom to pick your battles. The intimidation factor was an effective deterrent.

Reb had learned the process of a bear marking territory by observing the older bears. They would scratch trees, leaving marks as fingerprints. It served as notification to others that they had been there, and the space was spoken for. The observer could tell the size of the one doing the marking by the height of the mark on the tree. This was the determining factor as to whether it was wise to challenge the area in question. One of the other ways of marking was by bites in the tree. It was wise for a smaller bear to stay away and find an alternative area.

All the efforts showed a strong commitment made by the animals to protect their families and community. But now it was threatened by humans. There had to be a way to share space together without so much destruction.

These were subjects that Reb often discussed with his friend Storm. As they had grown up in the forest, Reb and Storm had remained good friends. They had been a reliable source of encouragement for one another. It was good to acknowledge that even bears had some dismal days. They knew each other so well that they knew when to intervene or when to refrain from getting involved.

There were many things that Reb admired about Storm's maturity. Storm had become a master tree climber, and he was superb at his hunting skills. Even though Storm was the younger of the two, he had already fathered several cubs. Storm still respected Reb's advice about cubs even though he did not have any of his own. He still had wisdom that was extremely beneficial.

Storm equally admired the work he saw Reb doing in the forest community. He had watched Reb's dedication to keeping the forest safe and beautiful for all the forest animals. Storm appreciated that the efforts being made could have long-lasting benefits for his cubs and all the forest animals for generations to come.

The forest landmarks and history that Reb and Storm shared in Gua were some of the things they hoped future generations would experience. The joy that it brought them was something everyone, whether animal or human, should enjoy. They both strongly believed that nature was designed for all creatures to enjoy freely.

Most of the bears in the woodlands were in their age group. They mostly learned survival skills when they were growing up at their home. They continued to implement those things while also looking out for one another.

Because of the destruction of much of the forest, it required some innovative alternatives. Many of the skills they had learned were no longer effective. They would sometimes have to travel closer to town in search of food. This brought them close to human residential areas. It was not a desirable scenario. The bears were not purposely destroying property, but they searched in areas to gather food for survival.

The humans often had fruit and vegetable gardens in their yards. Reb particularly enjoyed the fresh produce. He would try hard to gather the fruits that had fallen on the ground and not disturb the ones still on the vines. Oftentimes, he could just remove a lid from the garbage can in the yard and consume the food that had been thrown away. This was not a lasting solution for the animals or the humans.

Reb wished that he could have a meeting with the humans like he had had with the cougar and the tiger. He hoped that they could have comparable results. The lasting results from the forest had been more than they could imagine. The forest animals had come to an order particularly regarding housing. It did not interfere with their natural animal instinct but enhanced their mutual respect.

Reb had noticed that the living distance between the animals and the humans was measurably smaller. People were building homes near the animals' woodland homes. Animals were being forced from their natural habitat. Bear sightings were becoming more frequent with humans. There was an uneasiness and uncomfortable feeling developing throughout Gua. The Gua that so many people loved was changing. Because of fear, panicked decisions were made that often caused harm to one another.

There had recently been the loud noise of big trucks in the area. Not only was it producing lots of dust, but it was also producing disturbing noises almost every day. The nice, clean air was becoming increasingly polluted. During one of the late afternoons when the bears were out at the river catching fish, there was a caravan of construction trucks traveling by. One of Storm's sons was spooked by the loud noise and panicked. He froze in his tracks. The truck driver interpreted that to mean he was refusing to move and was about to attack him. He made the decision to use the truck as a weapon and hit the bear at an accelerated speed. Just as the truck swerved to hit the bear, Storm ran to push his son out of the path. He succeeded, but Storm was grazed by the truck on his hind legs. He lay on the ground momentarily, but he was able to move fast enough on his injured leg to prevent additional injury. The other bears at the river quickly helped Storm to safety. When he arrived back at the den, he realized he had a broken leg. Though he was in excruciating pain, he knew it could have been worse. He nearly lost his life, but he was happy to save his son.

It took weeks for Storm to get better, but he had a limp from his injury. He could not move as fast, but he was grateful to be alive.

LIVE FAST *before your clock strikes* **12**

Reb was notified of this incident and immediately came to the aid of his friend Storm. He was more determined than ever to spearhead the needed change in the forest. This should not have happened and should never happen again.

Reb sent out the word that all animals should gather at the base of the tree for an important meeting about humans on the next day. The tree had become a symbol for change. Like the tree planted by the water, they shall not be moved.

Reb knew he would get great responses, because many of the animals had been asking about the progress being made with protecting the forest. They shared Reb's concern. They knew that if anyone could do it, Reb was the one. The animals did not disappoint. They showed up in large numbers.

Reb began with the health update on Storm for the benefit of those who had not heard of the incident. When he shared the improvement of Storm, the animals erupted into a loud cheer. It set the tone of the need for lasting change to prevent further aggression from humans.

The sounds could be heard all over Gua. Many of the residents and tourists were alarmed. They wondered what was happening in the forest with all the animals. There were distinct sounds from so many different animal sources. They had not seen or heard anything like this before.

The residents encouraged law enforcement to investigate the source of the loud noises and to let the community know if it was safe to stay there.

In the meantime, under the tree, Reb began to hear suggestions from the animals. One suggestion was to destroy all the construction equipment so the workers could not continue to build. Another suggested surrounding the trees and threatening the workers. There were other suggestions, but the one agreed on by the majority was a large animal protest. They had never had a protest against humans, but they had been successful in gathering the animals for common causes. Because of their determination, they felt they could pull it off.

They did not have the ability to write letters as a petition or send a spokesperson with demands. Therefore, they had to determine the best way to communicate their concerns.

On Monday morning, they would all gather at the river. There would be some from every species in the forest. Even the water animals would participate. They all would come up to the surface of the water to show unity with the land animals. When the workers came in to work, they would be greeted by a tapestry of every species in their splendor as far as their eyes could see.

As scheduled, on Monday morning, the gathering started at 1:00 a.m. By 6:00 a.m., all the animals were in place. Now the wait was on for the workers to come.

LIVE FAST before your clock strikes 12

At 7:00 a.m., the dust clouds began to show up in the sky. The trucks were en route. There was a long caravan of yellow trucks with bold black letters: "SELIL ELLIV Construction."

It was not the words the animals could read, but they knew it was not a good sign but one of destruction. There was a dreadful feeling of anticipation. Reb did not know what the company could do to them. He hoped he had not put the animals in danger.

The trucks stopped far away from the river. They then started to drive beside one another to create a circle. They soon had the animals all fenced in with the big yellow trucks. It had become a stand-off situation.

This was the position for about one hour, and then the choppers were flying overhead. There were camera flashes going off and megaphones exuding loud noises. There were television interruptions with special reports. This was disturbing to the animals, but they would not move.

In the meantime, back in downtown Gua, tourists were being evacuated, and residents were being told to stay inside.

Some of the largest animals stepped out in front and slowly moved toward the trucks. Reb appeared from the middle of the group. He walked directly up to the middle of the circle. He knew he did not speak their language. Neither did they speak his language, but he had to find a way to communicate.

He carried a plank of wood on his back. It was his way of communicating that they were taking his shelter to cover him.

He then dropped the wood and picked it up with his mouth. That was his way of saying, "You are destroying our livelihood of food." He dropped the wood with a loud bang. It was his way of saying, "You are destroying us with your hunting."

Reb then stood tall on two legs. He began to grunt, moan, and bark to indicate he felt threatened.

After about twelve minutes of his full presentation, Reb lay down on the ground, indicating subordination and that he did not want to fight for dominance.

All of this was being captured by the cameras. All Gua was watching this unfold in real time within the comfort of their homes.

The strangest thing was that the humans understood what was being communicated by Reb.

The phones began to ring at the news stations. No one had ever seen such an elegant method of communication between a bear and humans.

Monetary donations and suggestions for protecting the animal community of Gua were being offered. There were residents that agreed with the animals. They had long been concerned that Gua was losing much of the appeal that had driven the tourism. The animals deserved to be safe.

After another hour, the trucks began to retreat. They turned around and traveled back to where they came from.

The political governing body of Gua decided to call an emergency meeting to discuss these new developments.

LIVE FAST *before your clock strikes* **12**

The animals retreated to their respective homes with a feeling of accomplishment. They had success for now. But how long would it last?

Reb had many things happening in his life. The change of events brought an optimism he had not seen. He decided that his time to start a family had now come. The upcoming breeding season would be his season as well. Just as he planned, Reb fathered two cubs the next winter.

Dran's Relocation and Exploring New Horizons

Dran could not believe he was technically an adult—though to most, it was pretty obvious by looking at him that he was still a child at heart. When he looked in the mirror, he could still see many of his childish features. Other than the few extra pounds, he did not feel particularly different.

He had finally stopped his growth spurt, which was exhilarating for him, because he was tired of people constantly asking him his height or whether he was a basketball player. They were usually taken aback when he replied that he only played musical instruments.

It was not the physical changes that Dran noticed most. It was the responsibilities of adulthood. Having to pay his own way and provide for himself was a shocking reality check for Dran. Monies never seemed to go quite as far when they came from his pockets. It was strange that he had never thought about money when he had lived at home with his parents. Though he could ask his parents for assistance, he was determined to figure things out on his own. He had the ability to adjust as he needed to whatever his current situation was. He learned to be resourceful but not completely satisfied. He was constantly striving to move forward and do better.

LIVE FAST before your clock strikes 12

Dran had lived his life as a free-spirited person and did not choose to worry about very many things. If it did not work for him the first time, he would reattempt or find a new endeavor. This philosophy had gotten him through some tough times, but he managed to come out on the other side successfully.

To accomplish the objectives he was so passionate about required him to move forward even with risk and sometimes fear. He knew he would not be pleased with himself if he did not persist. He did not want to live with regrets. There was a noticeable tenacity in him often recognized by his friends.

He had pursued a post–high school education. He was certain that the arts and entertainment were his areas of strength. Therefore, he pursued those studies during his college career. The curriculum would help him fulfill his dreams and purpose.

His love for entertainment and music took precedence over any other profession. While pursuing this career, he often accepted less-desirable jobs to meet his expense obligations. He accepted those situations as part of the process, and they were merely temporary stops to success.

While in college, he continued to widen his friendship circle. He met people from all levels of society. They were of all ethnicities and beliefs, yet they dwelled in peacefulness. They did not agree with one another 100 percent of the time, but there was a resolve and willingness to respect one another and remain open to learning.

He had many opportunities to travel with some of those friends. His palate expanded by trying many different ethnic foods. This made clear why there were a few extra pounds, but the food was delicious and very much worth the bulge.

The trips with his friends were a continuation of the love of travel he had developed as a child. His parents would often take him and his siblings on vacations with exciting landmarks and attractions. Sometimes, they would even allow them to bring a friend on their ventures. He always started with making room for Benno. When they did not take friends, his parents would often bring a babysitter so that they could venture out for adult time.

Now that travel was more selective, since it was self-sponsored, he chose very wisely. If it were a place he really wanted to go, he would set aside his money until he reached the amount required. It made him appreciate the sacrifices his parents had made over the years.

Dran was honing his entertainment skills every chance he got as a freelancer. Doors of opportunity continued to open, and he was well received by his audiences. He found that there were people willing to assist in helping him achieve his goals. They were encouraging to him. During this time, he continued to learn the insider's information about the industry.

Dran would continue to frequent Gua as often as he could. When there was a break from work or entertainment, he would return to the area. He enjoyed seeing family and friends, and he still loved the atmosphere of Gua. There was nothing like the fresh, crisp air of home.

There were a couple of his favorite restaurants there. Each time he returned home, he would stop by to visit the staff. He was always treated like a town celebrity. He was never allowed to pay for his meals, and he could eat as much as he wanted. It was their pleasure to serve him complimentarily. He would often visit there for two to three hours. He laughed, talked, and caught up on all the latest happenings in Gua. When he departed the restaurant, he would give big bear hugs to everyone and leave with his signature departure: "Ciao—until the next time! This will keep you."

One weekend, while Dran was visiting Gua, he attended a church service then stopped by the restaurant. He did not want to eat there, because his family was preparing a big meal. After the meal, he was going back to his house.

While waiting at the restaurant, he received a phone call from a friend. Though the friend knew it was a huge favor, he asked Dran to assist him in a drive to a town called Atsu. He was scheduled to go there on a job assignment. If things went well, it could be a permanent relocation. His friend knew of Dran's adventurous spirit and thought it just might be possible he would say yes.

As exciting and tempting as it was, Dran expressed his regrets and wished his friend a safe trip.

They promised to stay in touch with one another. There was disappointment, but his friend had no problem accepting Dran's decision. He knew Dran had many other things going on in his life. He was proud that Dran would honor his prior commitments. Dran left for Gua that evening after dinner as scheduled. When he returned to his home, he kept thinking about Atsu. He did not know much about it, so he searched for information. While reading about the town, he felt like he was reading about Gua. Atsu had a similar mountain range, natural beauty, and a variety of wildlife. He loved Gua, and the more he learned about Atsu, the more he felt he would really love a city with so much in common. There was not a big clock in the downtown area, but there were a few of the same stores that were in Gua.

The curiosity that had always driven Dran was compelling him to accept that adventure with his friend. That night was a restless one for Dran. He could not get Atsu off his mind. This could be the opportunity of a lifetime. He had never shied away from trying new things, and this was no exception.

The next day, he went to work and asked for a two-week leave. He made a convincing case with his supervisor. It did have an ounce of truth in it. Whatever was said, it worked. Dran was granted his request.

He was excited to call his friend when he got home. To his surprise, his friend had already reached Atsu. He had decided to fly after he could not find a second driver. No worries, though, his friend said. "If you can buy your own plane ticket, come on to Atsu. You can stay with me." This was music to Dran's ears. He announced his plans to his family, bought his plane ticket, and packed his bags.

    Three days later, Dran stepped on the grounds of Atsu. It was as beautiful as he imagined. For a minute, he felt like he was back in Gua. The comparison of the two cities was uncanny. There was the breathtaking mountain range and the streaming blue waters at the lakes. He considered them sister cities.

    Dran reflected on all his years of travel. He was reminded that there are similarities between people and places wherever you go. He thought about his middle school summer internship, where there were even more eerie resemblances and likenesses.

    Dran began to immerse himself in his new area. His friend was busy with his new job, so Dran would venture out on his own. He felt safe there.

    He was delighted to learn of the excellent and thriving arts and entertainment community. He certainly felt right at home. The move seemed to be a smart choice for him. He was watching opportunities unfold in an expedient manner. Atsu had something there for him.

    Dran accepted a job at a restaurant called Notes & Jokes. That name certainly sounded like the right place for him. Because of his background in entertainment, he quickly found himself in demand. His name circulated throughout the city and the surrounding areas. He was the new kid on the block, but he was making waves.

He quickly became a great asset to the company. Business was booming as patrons frequented the location. Lines were formed outside the restaurant with wait times over an hour. It was difficult to accommodate the crowds, and many would leave and try again on another day.

Management searched for ways to handle the influx of customers. For the first time ever, they decided to start accepting reservations. That solution was a minor help temporarily. The new problem only grew, because the reservations were for the sections of the restaurant serviced by Dran. It was not fair to the other employees; however, they could not compete with the magnetism of Dran. The struggle continued until finally, Dran was moved from serving and given a permanent position as an in-house entertainer.

He did thirty minutes on stage every hour from 3:00 p.m. to 9:00 p.m. Finally, Dran was doing what he loved most. He received many outstanding standing ovations and accolades. He had become one of the best things that had happened at Notes & Jokes.

He was so grateful for the invitation from his friend to come to Atsu. Things were going well for Dran.

At one of Dran's shows, he noticed a young lady sitting in a booth all alone. After quite some time had passed, he noticed no one joined her at the booth. He was appalled that she would use the entire seating area when there were people outside waiting to come in. The counter stools had a couple of empty spaces. She could sit there and free up that booth for a larger party. The thing that was even more appalling was the fact that she sat through two additional shows. Still, no one joined her.

He was pleased, however, that she was very engaged in his delivery. She laughed and cheered throughout the evening. She could be heard by all the other patrons. There were some segments when she even slammed her fist on the table with laughter and big screams. She was enjoying herself tremendously.

Dran was puzzled by her prolonged stay, and he was curious as to who she was. After the third set, he began to walk around and greet some of the patrons. When he reached her booth, he extended his hand to her and introduced himself. "Good afternoon," he said. "I am Dran the man, and who do I have the pleasure of greeting?"

With a melting smile, she replied softly, "Hi, my name is Mia."

She invited him to take a seat opposite her. He complied with that invitation, and their conversation started. Those thirty minutes went fast, but Dran was so engrossed that he missed the call for the next show. The manager eventually found him and reminded him he needed to be on stage. With slight reluctance, he conformed to the summons.

Dran had been successful in getting Mia's contact information. He was able to put that information to use as soon as his

9:00 p.m. show ended. At 9:45, he called Mia by phone. After the first ring, she answered, "Hi, this is Mia."

From the beginning, Dran and Mia spent lots of time together. While learning things about one another, Dran came to realize what an encouragement Mia was to him. She would often seek ways to help him and make his stay in Atsu smoother.

In conversations with one another, Mia finally confided that her night at his show was a work assignment. She was a writer and a reporter. There had been so much buzz about his performance that she was to investigate his phenomenon. She did not want to draw attention to herself, so she kept the booth solo. She shared that she was also a cousin of the Notes & Jokes owner.

Dran was surprised to hear the details of the night they met. He felt he was somewhat violated and a little deceived, because she had not told him the details that evening. When all was said and done, he understood it was her job. He was able to put it all behind him and accept that it was just an interesting part of their story.

There had been an immediate attraction to Mia. She was a person that checked off many of the imaginary boxes that he had in his head. She was what he was searching for in a life partner. He could imagine them sharing a life together.

The friend that brought Dran to Atsu had been introduced to his wife by Mia. It was an unbelievable fate that they both would start their families there. Gua and Atsu came together to make them complete.

The relationship progressed quickly, and in twelve months, Dran and Mia were a married couple. Within a few years, they had two boys.

Dran and Mia opened their own club, where Dran was the weekend headliner. He was proud to host other up-and-coming entertainers at his club on amateur nights. It was a tremendous success.

Mia continued to do her writing and reporting throughout Gua and the surrounding areas.

Life was moving fast for Dran and his family. He was happy, he was financially secure, and he was surrounded by people who loved him. He was often recognized by the local community when he was around town with his family. He was living his dream.

There was, however, something missing within Dran. Having success was something he always wanted, but he could not share it with his extended family in Gua. He had not been home in a few years. The phone calls were great, but face-to-face would be so much better. He missed giving those big bear hugs.

It had been a long time, but Dran had to admit to himself that he was homesick. He wanted to see his Gua family and friends. He wanted to eat at his favorite restaurants, attend worship services, and walk the streets of beautiful Gua.

There would be a family reunion in a few months. This would be the perfect time to see lots of people at once and introduce his new family to his Gua family. He had spoken so highly of his home being so much like Atsu. Mia and the boys were excited to finally see this place.

Dran called his family to confirm the dates of the reunion. Subsequently, he reserved their airline tickets and hotel accommodations. And now, yet another countdown began! He did not do another calendar, but every day was checked off in his head.

LIVE FAST *before your clock strikes* **12**

Encounter at the Strawberry Patch

Gua was only one week away after a five-year hiatus for Dran. There had not been any intention to stay away that long, but time had passed surprisingly quickly.

So much had happened in Dran's life since his move to Atsu. Every aspect of his life had made major strides. With his expanded family and his thriving career, his Gua family had quite a bit to adjust to.

He accepted that much in the life of his Gua family had also changed. He hoped that he would be able to recognize them both physically and emotionally.

The euphoria was intense as Dran prepared with his family for the big family reunion. He was confident that once his family saw the city of Gua, they would agree with all he had shared about his home.

Their luggage packing was done as lightly as they could. He had already been told that his Gua family had many gifts for them to take home, especially for the boys. He was not excited at all about the gifts, but he was thrilled to see his family again.

On the day of the plane ride to Gua, Dran attempted to prepare the boys for the flight. He even remembered some of the tips from Mr. Bear that he had received while traveling on his summer internship many years ago. It was the boys' first flight, so he certainly related to the anxiety they could be experiencing. Those tips were good for him, so he was optimistic that they would benefit the boys.

After a smooth ride, the plane landed at 10:30 a.m. One of his cousins was there to greet them and chauffeur them to the hosting hotel. Seeing his cousin sent a rush of adrenaline all over his body. The excitement was unmistakable. They hugged with the greatest grip they could muster. The cousin appreciated the big bear hug that he had missed all those years. Dran felt genuine love and a sincere welcome. He was so happy to be back home.

LIVE FAST *before your clock strikes* 12

He did an introduction to his family, and off they went to load the vehicle. On the way, his cousin slipped in a few funny stories about growing up with Dran. It kept Mia and the boys laughing. The boys could not imagine their dad doing some of the mischievous ploys that his cousin was sharing with them.

As they rode through the streets of Gua, Mia was captivated by the beauty of this city… Dran had not done it justice when he described it to them, though he had tried. The streets of Gua brought back so many cherished memories for Dran.

As they arrived at the intersection of Broad Street and Forest Street, Dran asked his cousin to pull the car over at the first available parking space. He had to make sure that this was the first stop for his family. It was important to Dran that this was their first picture. A picture by the clock was considered the official welcome of Gua. He wanted his family to experience it.

Most visitors made it their first stop in town. The nostalgia of that majestic clock never grew old.

As they posed for their picture, the clock bonged twelve at the same time the finger snapped. It was a synchronized movement that was in no way planned. It was a sound heard across the city with the mountain echo. Dran's cousin commented that the clock must know he had returned. Dran's reply was, "The clock is probably reminding me I need to hurry, because I still have a lot to do." So they resumed their trip. Mia and the boys said that the clock had given them a cool and memorable welcome! It was just one of those unexplainable mysteries of Gua. While growing up in Gua, Dran experienced many baffling phenomena.

During the three-day reunion, there would be other visits downtown and more cousin pictures standing by the iconic clock. But for now, his family had the picture that would be placed on their mantle when they returned home.

Continuing the ride allowed Dran the opportunity to show his family many landmarks that were a significant part of his growing up there. Mia was struck with the similarities of Gua and Atsu. It was eerie to witness. She understood why Dran missed being in this beautiful city. She was fast gaining a fondness for it herself.

When they arrived at the hotel, the family was already gathering. He hurried to process his hotel stay then quickly rejoined his family. There were hugs, pictures, and refreshments all happening simultaneously. Dran was beside himself. He was grinning from ear to ear. As a bonus, he was tasting some of his cousin's delicious dishes. The appetizers were so delicious, he could not wait to see what the main course would taste like.

From a distance, Mia perceived that she had never seen Dran this happy. She was happy that they had decided to come to the reunion. She was meeting new family members, and Dran was rekindling relationships. They socialized for a few more hours and then excused themselves to rest for the next day. The trip itself was exhausting. They could all benefit from a good night's rest.

The next day was the day of the picnic. Dran saw even more cousins. Many of them he had not seen since childhood. Of course, they looked different, but there was an unmistakable family resemblance.

Many of the men had come in early that morning to prepare the meats for barbecue and grilling. Many of the women were preparing the side dishes.

The major surprise at the picnic was churning fresh strawberry ice cream. It would be their special dessert. There were a group of volunteer men scheduled to go to the strawberry patch and pick enough to make several gallons of ice cream. Their instructions were to pick the plumpest and juiciest ones to make this batch the best ever.

This had been a traditional activity from previous reunions. It was a bonding time for the men and somewhat of a rite of passage. It was hard to claim membership in the family if you never experienced the strawberry patch. After all these years, Dran was surprised the patch was still bearing strawberries.

The necessary attire was provided. They would wear long-sleeved shirts, long pants, and a straw hat. They had to wear close-toed shoes. This was all to keep them protected from the bugs and thorns. For extra protection, they were rubbing alcohol and turpentine over their bodies. With all these layers of protection, the bugs and mosquitoes did not stand a chance. At least, that was their desire.

There was a twelve-man volunteer group. They all grabbed a pail and began the one-mile walk to the strawberry patch. They passed familiar sites as well as some new constructions. They laughed and reminisced about growing up in Gua. The stories kept coming from different ones. Some of the cousins had slightly different versions from the others, but it all brought about jovial laughs.

One of the stories they all agreed on was picking strawberries as a child. Their pails would never get full because they ate twice as many as they saved. Though they tried to protect themselves, they managed to be bitten by red bugs and mosquitos. To make matters worse, they usually had a stomachache. This was a total consensus. They remembered these facts the same.

They wished their children could enjoy some of those same ventures, because that was how incredible, lasting memories were made for them.

Within the last half mile, they passed more familiar sites, including a residential area. They remembered some of the people that used to live there, but the occupancy had changed for most of them. As they got closer, they saw a lady sitting on the porch in a rocking chair. They were not sure if they knew her, but they exchanged pleasantries. When she responded, Dran immediately recognized her voice. She screamed out to them, saying, "Who are these farmers walking down the road?" With a glaring look, she screamed out, "Dran, is that you?" He replied with a resounding yes!

How could he ever forget her? She had been his favorite teacher. He would never forget the impact she'd had on his life. She had believed in him at an early age, and he attributed much of his success to his connection to her. It was common for her to seek information about her former students. Therefore, she had heard that he had relocated and was now married with children. She also heard of his career success. She was so proud of him but never dreamed he would be walking past her house in a farmer's outfit.

They shared with her the mission they were on to get strawberries for homemade ice cream.

She was impressed that they were prepared for the tiny bugs and mosquitoes, but her question was, "How prepared are you for the crawling and larger animals?" Dran thought that this was the kind of question a dedicated and concerned teacher would ask.

She shared that she had seen snakes in the area, and less than two weeks ago, she had seen two bear cubs on the opposite side of the road. She cautioned him to be observant and above all, be careful.

They said their goodbyes, and, in typical Dran form, he reached over and gave her a big bear hug.

When they left her yard, Dran thought of what she had said. When he observed a long stick on the road, he verified that it was not a snake, and he picked it up to use in the strawberry patch. He knew it would not fend off a bear or even stop a snake, but it would keep noise as he hit the bushes. Maybe that would scare them away.

He paused for a minute to ask his cousins if they were okay to continue. Most of them verified they were, but they needed to speed things up. They had lost some of their time visiting. In addition, they now knew of additional critters to watch for.

One cousin threw out a suggestion of going to the store to buy the best strawberry ice cream they could find. Then they could skip the strawberry picking. This did not go over well with the rest of the cousins, so they set their sights on the patch and kept going.

When they reached the patch, they could smell the freshness of the berries. The aroma was enticing, but they wondered what else was lurking in the pasture. Dran used his stick to beat down the bushes and open the paths. He and the cousins were remarkably surprised that the patch was relatively clear going in. That made them think that there had been frequent visitors at the strawberry patch.

As they glanced around the field, there seemed to still be many strawberries remaining. There were some bare areas where someone had gone before them for picking, but overall, they were plentiful.

They agreed that it should not take long to fill their pails. They also agreed to control their eating so they would accomplish their goal much faster. With twelve men, they should have enough for several gallons in an hour or less.

The men got busy picking. They kept their eyes scanning their surroundings, and they were pleased they saw or heard nothing out of the ordinary.

Within forty-five minutes, they had the twelve buckets half full.

They had been gone a little longer than planned, so they decided that was enough. They were waiting for them to start churning back at the hotel.

They all headed toward the path leading out. When they were close to being out, Dran remembered his stick. He had propped it against a tree while he was bending. He asked them to hold up while he ran back to get it.

As he reached to grab the stick, there were hands climbing down the tree directly above his.

He was startled and jumped. He did not scream but slowly backed away. From the tree emerged a full-sized bear. The bear locked his eyes in a stare directly into Dran's eyes. Those eyes were remarkably familiar.

The bear uttered a soft whisper and smiled. As Dran continued to walk away, the bear raised his right paw and waved it at Dran. Dran backed his way out of the patch with the stick in his hand. To his surprise, he was not frightened at all.

He rejoined his cousins, and they began the walk back to enjoy the picnic and churn the delicious strawberry ice cream.

He did not share the bear encounter with his cousins. They would never believe him.

VIVIAN WARD NEWTON

It's Six O'Clock

Oh, how time is ticking;
Can I get it all done?
I've had my time of misery,
but wow, have I had fun.
I dotted *I*'s
and I've crossed *T*'s;
You've seen me disembark,
but my bucket list was lengthy,
and it is already six o'clock.

A Time to Transform and Become:
ATTRIBUTES AT 12:01 P.M. TO 06:00 P.M.

This is the time that many begin to feel like adults.
There is an accepting of responsibilities.
There is an effort to shift purpose to others and seek deeper connections.
Thoughts of being good spouses and parents take precedence.
There is a hunkering down of work.
Career achievements are made.
Life drifts into seasons of change often seen in late adulthood.
The roles shift as their children grow up.
There is a letting go of long-standing roles.
This could lead to altered family dynamics.
There are preparations to become empty nesters.
There are often reflections and acceptance of life's impermanence.
This is often a time of significant life alterations.
This time of life may bring an identity crisis and a great feeling of loss.
There may be anxiety about the future.
It is crucial for self-reflection, finding comfort in change, expressing gratitude, and mentoring the younger generation.
Opportunities arise to embrace a more peaceful pace while appreciating the rich tapestry of past experiences.

LIFE OF REB AND DRAN:
6:00 P.M. TO 11:59 P.M.

Reb Helping Others

As Reb was getting older, he assessed his life to evaluate the most important contributions to his legacy. His ultimate desire was to leave the forest even better than it was the generation he was born. He thought of the impact he would have by sharing life skills with the younger cubs. He felt qualified to expound on all his many ventures, both good and bad. Some would be skill information, and some would be for cautionary warnings. The town and inhabitants of Gua deserved all the efforts from every citizen to share what was helpful to preserve its beauty.

By now, he had two cubs of his own. He hoped that they would avoid many of the pitfalls he encountered in his life. Through trial and error, he had experienced many hits and countless misses, but all was not lost. The lessons learned were priceless. He hoped to be an example to his offspring as well as a positive influence on all the other cubs.

LIVE FAST before your clock strikes 12

The years in the forest had earned Reb a well-founded level of respect. There was an aura about him that would leave many of the younger ones in awe. Some of the younger bears would scurry away when Reb was nearby, because they were so intimidated by his presence.

He walked with authority, and he spoke with clarity and preciseness. He made a difference in the forest, and the animals had a high respect for his many efforts. He had made major strides in the bear community.

There had always been stories that circulated throughout the forest of Reb's reputation from earlier years. They had been told of his unusual birth and the labels that many other animals assigned to him. It had been established after his birth that others believed that he was unique among the bears and that he would do some remarkable things in his life.

They had seen many of the predictions come true, and they had a strong suspicion there was more to come. The cubs considered themselves fortunate to be born at a time to experience some of Reb's life and share a small part of his lasting legacy.

He had reached the adult weight of seven hundred pounds. His presence alone intimidated most of the other animals. There had been occasions when he used his size to his advantage, and without striking a blow, he had triumphant wins.

Because of his size, he could not move around as fast as he once had. But he could still outpace most of the other animals.

Reb had settled most of his fears by now. He kept a regular routine of rising before sunrise and bedding down an hour or two after sunset.

He still attempted to avoid contact with humans, so on most occasions, he would go searching during the nights to decrease his run-in chances.

Much of his time was spent foraging for prey and fishing for salmon. Salmon had become his favorite meal. He would have it as much as possible. With his huge size came a huge appetite. He also loved eating fruits, berries, and grasses. They were mostly used as a snack for him, but sometimes he ate so many that it equated to a full meal.

Besides eating, he would often gather some of the younger bears around and share his knowledge of grizzly history. They enjoyed hearing Reb expound on things he had learned over the years. He always made his presentations very entertaining, so there was usually a big audience. The cubs were attentive, because though it was entertaining, it was also valuable information to increase their chances of survival in the forest.

In his teaching, Reb emphasized the importance of eating huge meals during the summer months. He explained the need to build great fat reserves and that it was necessary to survive the winter hibernation period. They were delighted to know there was a legitimate reason to overeat.

LIVE FAST before your clock strikes 12

One of Reb's favorite discussions was the actual history of the grizzly bear. He felt strongly that the bears should know where they came from and the contributions of their ancestors.

He explained that they were grizzlies, but also, they were part of the brown bear species. There are two subspecies of a brown bear, the Kodiak bear, which lives only on the Kodiak Archipelago, and the grizzly bear, which lives everywhere else. He emphasized the importance of acknowledging and appreciating their relatives.

One of the bear cubs asked, "How did the grizzly bear get its name?" With self-reliance, Reb gave a detailed commentary of the name origin.

It was because their brown fur can be tipped with white. This gave them a grizzled look, especially when backlit by the sun. It was a mix of dark and white hair.

Reb felt proud that he was providing needed information. In some cases, the cubs had not received training at home. In other cases, the training was inadequate. Reb had seen a need, and he vigorously attempted to fill it.

As a result of Reb's extensive preparation, this generation of cubs were some of the most intelligent packs that ever lived in Gua.

A great challenge was proposed by Reb. He strongly emphasized how important it was to protect one another. The grizzly population was dwindling due to the lower birth rates, human land development, and bear hunting. There was a risk of extinction. None of the bears wanted to hear those statistics, but they knew Reb was being truthful with them. They, too, had seen many of the changes in Gua.

It had placed the bears in a tricky situation. There were human-created food sources available, such as garbage cans and dumpsters. It caused an unnatural dependency on human foods. This was neither beneficial nor sustainable.

If the bears were then relocated forcefully, they would not survive against the least-domesticated bear, because they had not learned to hunt. They could not survive without food. The long-term effect was bear extinction.

Reb even quoted something he heard from a human that says, "If you give a man a fish, you've fed him for the day. If you teach a man to fish, you've fed him a lifetime." This statement was relevant in their community as well.

He reminded them of the forces of oppression. The obvious were the humans, but there were others that fell into the categories of the hunter and the hunted within the animal kingdom. He cautioned the cubs not to get complacent but to remain cautious.

These Reb lessons and examples were practical and useful for day-to-day living.

Reb was an excellent teacher and was just who the community needed. Being around him was like being at a bear university. He was a mentor and an example for all that chose to listen.

LIVE FAST before your clock strikes 12

The animal community was adjusting to the changes being made in Gua. The construction had ceased. They no longer saw the big yellow trucks with the "Selil Elliv" emblem stirring up dust clouds.

The governing body of Gua had been active in putting the order in place. It had designed a plan and passed a new city ordinance that protected the animals. All hunting was banned. Many of the city landmarks were labeled as natural or historic monuments. Therefore, they could not be altered. There were zoning laws put in place to prevent the building of new structures within five miles of the animal habitats.

There was still lots of conversation about the monumental animal protest orchestrated by their spokesbear, Reb. They had all witnessed the greatest animal revolt ever seen in history. It had all been recorded and documented.

Reb was proud of this major accomplishment, but he knew there was still work to be done. He was not boastful, and he did not take all the credit for its success. Everyone had participated. It would now take everyone agreeing to work together to maintain what they had accomplished.

This was done strictly on behalf of the animals. It established that humans and nonhumans were of equal importance.

The greatest accomplishment for all the animals was now having human support. Because of the funds raised and those continuing to come in, they were able to see the Protective Animal Sanctuary created.

It was under the leadership of a human advocate named Dran. It was a designated area within the confines of Gua in a breathtaking domain. The animals could live and be protected there for the rest of their lives.

If the animals preferred remaining in the wild forest, they would still have protection by the ordinances. No human could knowingly cause harm to them.

There was a greater accomplishment for both the humans and the animals. The animals had served as fitting examples for the world to see. They demonstrated what could be accomplished when the effort is made to come together for a common cause. The entire world witnessed the miracle of animals and humans compromising.

They were not concerned about what each animal looked like, how they smelled, what size they were, or the colors in their skin. They were not concerned about the language barrier between the animals and the humans.

There were a few things that embodied commonality from each species of animal. Yet there was no shortage of an ability to pinpoint differences. However, the greatest driving factor for success was the ability to put those differences aside and focus on the cause at hand. They all contributed to coming together as a whole. Their success was based on unity. Therefore, the change they were seeking became a reality that benefited them all.

LIVE FAST before your clock strikes 12

That was a lesson that permeated Gua and the world. Human universities analyzed the meaning. Social and religious organizations used it as examples to teach on caring and standing for your belief. Tolerance was being taught simultaneously across the world.

It made Gua an even greater attraction for tourists. It already had a reputation for its pristine landscape. It already had a reputation for its strange clock. But now, the reputation for the display of unity of the animals made it a mecca.

The clock on Broad Street and Forest Road was still the first photo landmark for the tourists, but the next one became the river where the animals had gathered in protest.

Reb had an established place at the sanctuary. He still spent time mentoring the other animals. He was a voice of reason in conflicts and other demanding situations. He was able to spend time with other animals and serve as a counselor for them.

As Reb interacted with the animals, he noticed that the animals were making more effort to communicate with one another. There was a genuine respect for diversity. There were still obstacles to overcome. Speaking the language was one of the biggest ones. Despite that, they found ways to communicate.

Young and old talked about the difference Reb made in the town of Gua. With the animal protest being seen across the world, they realized that Reb's bold act had changed the world. The things said about Reb at an early age had all come about. They had seen no other bear like him.

There was no doubt that in Reb's short years, he had accomplished impactful transformations that would change the world forever.

Dran Gives Back to Gua

The week's stay at the family reunion zoomed past. There were places that Dran wanted to show Mia and the boys. Unfortunately, he did not accomplish them all but was able to show some of the highlights and establishments. Time would not allow them to complete all their tours. He promised a more thorough excursion on their next trip to Gua.

His week's stay at the family reunion emphatically solidified his thoughts of moving back to Gua. It had been a time of reflection for Dran. It had stirred up some suppressed feelings he did not know he had. There seemed to be something in Gua left for him to do. Leaving the area brought a deep feeling of grief as he boarded the plane to go back to Atsu. He was not the only person feeling regretful. Mia and the boys hated to leave.

They had made impactful connections at the reunion. They felt welcome and right at home. The boys loved meeting and enjoying their cousins. They had been in constant contact since they had returned home. There had been a reoccurring discussion of the things they would do when they got back together. There was also an anticipation of meeting additional cousins that lived in nearby areas. The boys would have opportunities to experience some of the things Dad always talked about with them. He had made it hard not to await the explorations.

Dran wanted to be fair to Mia, because he was taking her from her family and the only home she had known. She, however, shared his excitement and told him so. As part of her humor, she had said to him, "There is a way in and a way out. If things do not work, they will take a different route." They laughed about it but decided to adopt this as their family's motto as it related to the move to Gua.

As they had promised, his family sent many gifts back home with them. One of them was a wall plaque with the name Gua in bold letters. The city name was being held by a large grizzly bear. They all thought it was the perfect gift to hang on the kitchen wall. They would see it every day, knowing that it would not be long before this would be their new residence. Dran was excited for the reminder of home, and of course, the bear reminded him of Benno.

He had enjoyed living in Atsu. The people and place were phenomenal. He thought about how blessed he was to have an opportunity to pursue his career dreams there, and he found it to be receptive enough for him to excel. He was even more blessed to start a family there. Had he not gone to Atsu, he would never have met Mia. Then he would not have his two boys, who were the joys of his life. He was forever grateful to his friend for inviting him there. Mia had also been instrumental in introducing his friend to his now-wife. Atsu had been great for them both.

All these factors were beneficial to him, but they still could never replace the love he had for the people of Gua. He wrestled with leaving a city that had been so good to him, yet he felt the only solution was to return to the place he loved so much.

There was nothing bad he could say about Atsu except that it was not Gua. Despite the likeness of the two cities, there was an aura in Gua that was not duplicable anyplace else. It was a resolve he had to make to himself that Gua was calling him back home.

Dran had stayed connected with the local news of Gua. He had been a newspaper subscriber ever since he relocated to Atsu. Between the family conversations by phone and his newspaper, he stayed well informed. He could hear of families' lives even down to the latest winner in the beautiful garden contest. With accessibility to national news, any major event would travel within minutes.

In Atsu, Dran had even seen the animal protest on television. It had warranted national news, so he had seen it unfold in real time, as did the rest of the world. While watching it on television, he remembered being on the phone with a play-by-play commentary.

He saved all the photographs that were printed in his subscribed newspaper. It had been the talk of the town in Atsu for many weeks afterward. When the Atsu residents heard it was

Dran's hometown, they would seek him out, as they hungered for the latest updates. It was common to hear people mention the animal phenomenon in their daily conversations. It had a life all its own. The talk died down, but it never disappeared.

Reb had thought of things he could do when he relocated to Gua. He never wanted to completely give up his entertainment work, but he ruled out opening a business. He would prefer to do periodic shows without a long-term commitment.

He had been able to sell his Atsu business to the Notes & Jokes owner as his second location.

Mia decided to continue her pursuits as a freelance writer and reporter. She had been offered a position on the local broadcast, which she graciously accepted. Gua would provide many interesting stories for her to share with the community.

Dran's family had always been involved in animal care. He had grown up in the veterinarian business owned by his father. His father was retiring, and he had offered Dran the opportunity to take over the business.

There were so many changes going on in Gua, Dran certainly wanted to be involved in the revitalization that was going on in the area. He had been fortunate enough to have financial success in his career while in Atsu. His move to Atsu years ago had proven to be a prosperous move for him. Now, he could come back home where his contributions to Gua were not driven by money. He felt that if he ever had to work a job, then the things that worked in Atsu would work in Gua. After all, they were almost sister cities.

Things all fell in place for their move. They waited for the most convenient time to relocate to Gua. The boys would be out of school in a few weeks, which was determined to be the ideal time. Their travels took a few days because of overnight stays on their journey. When Dran reached the city limits of Gua, there was an overwhelming feeling of peace. He knew this was where he needed to be at this time in his life.

Mia asked about riding through downtown so that they could take a picture with the clock. This would be their new welcome picture for their new home. Dran stopped and went to the trunk of his car for the camera. When he opened the trunk, the wall plaque of the grizzly bear holding the Gua sign fell on the ground. Dran was sure that he had packed the sign in a box so that it would not be damaged. He had no idea how it was now in the trunk and how it fell out. Mia confirmed that she had not placed it there. Neither had the boys handled it. He picked it up and laid it on top of the car until they took their picture. As they posed for the picture, the sign fell on the ground in the same spot it was before.

Mia and Dran busted out in laughter. She made the comment that there was no doubt they were in Gua. The strange acts continued. They took the picture and headed to their temporary home for the next few weeks. They would actively search for their permanent residence. He wanted to allow Mia the opportunity to learn more about the area before they agreed on the best place for their family.

As the family was active around Gua, they were greeted with sincere welcomes. The community residents offered any assistance they might provide to help them get settled. Within days of Dran's arrival back in Gua, he was approached by one of the town council members. He and Dran had been school classmates. Without any pressure or urgency, he shared the hopes that Dran would be a part of their administration. He knew Dran would be a great asset for the city. Dran did not respond except with a smile.

He reached to give Dran a big embrace, and Dran, as usual, offered his big bear hug. They both laughed, because they realized little had changed since the early years of their friendship.

Weeks passed, and Dran ran into him again at one of the downtown eateries. They agreed to share a table together, which would allow them a chance to talk. Though it was impromptu, many topics were discussed.

They discussed some of the changes going on within the city and the current needs. He asked Dran if he would consider serving on the animal sanctuary board. His duties would be to navigate governance and compliance issues. He felt Dran could do an exceptional job, considering his charisma and unconditional love for all living beings. He had been around animals most of his life, so his reputation preceded him. He was also very qualified professionally.

His friend remembered from years ago that Dran had a love for animals. He recalled the bus ride they had taken in elementary school to the reservation. They sat together on the bus and even shared their lunches. They talked about the little bear that kept following Dran through the glass partition. He even remembered Benno. He was more shocked to find out that Dran still had Benno on his nightstand in his bedroom.

Dran could not believe all the details his friend remembered, but it was wonderful to reminisce. He expressed his excitement at the possibility of accepting the job. He would go home, think about it, and discuss the time commitment with Mia. He promised to get back to his friend in a few days.

Dran did not know what he would spend his time doing in Gua, but this seemed like a perfect opportunity to acclimate him and his family back into the community. He had not even had a chance to look for a position. The position came looking for him. He thought it must have been meant to be.

He could not wait to get back and share the good news with Mia and the boys. The boys would love to spend time around the sanctuary. They were animal lovers like their dad.

It happened just the way Dran thought it would. The boys were jumping up and down, and Mia was grinning from ear to ear. She said that evidently, Gua had just been waiting for him to come back home. She had no doubt that he would do splendid work for the organization.

Dran and Mia spent the next few weeks looking for a home suitable for his family. He also wanted to be close to the sanctuary. They soon found and purchased a home midway between downtown and the animals. This was a perfect location for Dran to conveniently accomplish his daily obligations yet have a short commute from home.

Another especially important thing for Dran to do was to take Mia and the boys to see his middle school teacher. It was a divine visit. She shared many stories of Dran as a student. The boys had great laughs. It was hilarious imagining their dad as a young boy.

When they were about to leave, his teacher asked him for that big hug again, and she tried to big-hug him back. They laughed, because she could not even get her little arms around him. He felt good that she tried. Dran promised to stay in touch with her now that he was back in the area. He would take the family by for periodic visits. She was thrilled to have Dran and his family back and a part of her life.

Dran had adjusted to listening to the sounds of the old clock again. One of the things Dran really wanted to do was to have it fully restored. He was optimistic that the best technician that money could buy would be able to bring it back to its full glory. It had meant so much to so many people that Dran really wanted it to function properly. It had stood in that position for over one hundred years, and he wanted the clock repaired as the city was being revitalized.

The residents had reluctantly made the adjustments to the off time at twelve o'clock midnight. It would not strike at that time. Shortly after, it would readjust the hands a minute later to 12:01 a.m. It did not matter very much to most, because only a few people were on the streets at midnight.

Early the next morning, Dran met his friend downtown for breakfast. He would have the opportunity to share his plan about the clock. His friend was ecstatic to hear that this would be done without costing the city any funds. Dran was contributing all the expenses for the job.

They agreed to contact the leading clock repairer in the area. They were about six hours away. The company agreed to send a representative to give an estimate once they reviewed the job. Dran was not particularly concerned about the price, because it was something he had committed to doing. He wanted it for the residents of Gua.

The following Thursday, the representative's flight landed in Gua. He met at the councilor's office. They immediately drove down to the clock. The representative was extremely impressed with the uniqueness of the grand vintage timepiece. He had never seen anything like it. The pictures he had seen had not done it justice.

The craftsmanship was exceptional quality, with exquisite attention to detail. The representative knew it would be a delicate

LIVE FAST before your clock strikes 12

job, but he was confident the company could restore the accuracy of the original piece.

The representative stayed in town, and three others flew in the following day. A truck arrived with a long scapple, and several ladders were placed around the base of the clock.

Barriers were set up around the perimeters. Photographers were stationed out on the street to watch the delicate operation. They had long lenses on the camera, because they were not allowed within two hundred feet. There was silence required so that the workers would not be distracted.

When work began, a hush fell over the downtown area. Within two hours, they had taken the clockwork, the escarpment, the moving parts, the wheels and pinions, and the dial apart from the glass-enclosed facing. Meticulously, the clock was separated.

If you looked around, you could see tears falling from some of the residents. It was difficult to see the dismemberment of this special clock.

There were an additional two hours spent examining each piece and searching the cavities of every part of this clock. One of the workers broke the silence with a scream of the word, "Eureka." He had stumbled across a small piece of wood nestled in the back portion of the clock.

Cheers erupted from the people that were still there watching this undertaking. It was an amazing feeling for the worker to finally solve that mystery that had plagued this clock for so many years. The workers removed the wood piece and began the process of reassembling the clock.

Word began to spread that the clock had been repaired. People were excited and genuinely thankful to Dran for hiring the best technicians for the job. They were all anxious to watch the hands moving on the clock again. Many stayed until midnight to witness the first *bong* at midnight in nearly forty years.

At 6:00 p.m., there was surprisingly a roar emitted from the clock. The anticipated big *bong* did not happen. Another big hush settled over the crowd. Shortly afterward, you could hear screeching and moaning from the standing audience.

Now, they would wait until midnight to see if the clock would blow out a big *bong* at that time. They camped out on the street with chairs, blankets, and food as if it were a picnic. They waited patiently to hear the first midnight *bong* after forty years. They started a countdown at 11:55 p.m. When 11:59 p.m. came, they got louder. "Fifty-nine, fifty-eight, fifty-seven, fifty-six, fifty-five… ten, nine, eight, seven, six, five, four, three, two, one!" But again, the clock did what the clock had done for the last forty years. It skipped 12:00 a.m. There was, again, no midnight sound.

The people yelled at the technicians, but there was nothing anyone could do. They expressed their disappointment to one another and hoped that they would just leave the clock alone before they did additional damage. They all returned to their respective homes.

LIVE FAST before your clock strikes 12

By 12:30 a.m., the streets were empty, and things were back to normal. The technicians, council members, and residents all shut down and retired for the night.

When the council members met with Dran the next day, they decided to forfeit a repeat of the failed repair attempt.

Dran again offered to finance another clock repair company, but the council members turned the offer down. Dran was extremely disappointed. He felt he had given hope to the community that this could finally happen but had let them down. The community was in fact disappointed, but they did not blame Dran for the failure. He wondered if there was anyone who could solve the mystery of the clock.

The repair company was also disappointed. They had used all their expertise but did not get the job done. Therefore, they would not accept any funds from Dran or the council members since the effort had not been successful.

The mystique of Gua continued. How could a clock move uninterrupted for twenty-four hours per day for all these years? Then for the last almost forty years it lost the last minute of the day. Dran did not know how, but he knew he would keep searching until he found out.

Encounter at the Celebration

Dran's family was jubilant to have him back in Gua. They had already begun to plan family events where Dran could take part. They knew him to be a great facilitator, and though they did not want to monopolize his time, they had confidence he could contribute his sensible advice.

They could always look forward to his entertainment. He certainly knew how to enlist the audience for a guaranteed blissful time.

Dran was always willing to go the extra mile, but he had to be cautious about overcommitting. He had to keep a healthy balance with work and his family time.

He and Mia were both searching for activities in Gua. There were many sports games, festivals, and shows at a variety of venues within twenty miles. There were many choices of upcoming dates in that it was summer, and many businesses planned for family outings. It was difficult to choose the ones that he thought would be the most gratifying for his family.

His boys were extremely competitive in sports, so any activity that involved movement and scores was usually what they were most interested in. It was also a clever way to exert their built-up energy. He found that if he narrowed the choices down to two and let the boys pick one, it usually satisfied everybody.

They were enjoying all the things they participated in. He could not get enough of those Gua streets. He was often seen shopping downtown with Mia and the boys.

Mia had come to expect that an hour trip shopping could easily become a two- or three-hour stopover. Dran was going to spend lots of time running into acquaintances. The street conversations could sometimes be extremely long. Mia was patient, because she understood the pride the townspeople had in Dran. They were proud of his many accomplishments.

The boys were not always as patient as Mia. But there was nothing a good ice-cream cone could not fix. Most of the time the shopping trip ended with everyone benefiting and having an enjoyable time.

One of the biggest community festivals was coming soon. It was an annual celebration located by the river. It was centered around the anniversary of the animal protest. This year would be the third one since the animal and human confrontation. It had grown in population each year.

Dran and his family were attending for the first time since his return to Gua. He had seen on television the pageantry of this event. It had been a most impressive sight to witness. To now be there in person was a dream come true. As a bonus, he was a participant in planning the details. He also had the privilege to work on the grounds of this splendid event.

His job this year was monitoring the rides for overcrowding and keeping track of the gate entrance to ensure it did not exceed capacity. He was happy to accept these assignments, because he was able to handle those duties and still have fun with his family.

The festival had become a great fundraiser for the community. The proceeds raised were shared with local organizations. This year was especially exciting for Dran, because the proceeds would benefit some of the projects at the animal sanctuary.

Most of the participants, children and adults, would dress in their favorite animal costumes. Many people prepared all year, and their designs were increasingly elaborate. Some of the costumes looked like real animals. The furs and the paws were almost indistinguishable from the real thing. Some of the participants had practiced the animal gestures and almost perfected their movement.

There was a contest for the best-dressed animals, best-sounding animals, and the best human/pet lookalike.

The local high school bands would participate in the festival. It was one of the most talked-about highlights. They had learned to simulate with their instruments the sounds of many animals.

It was spectacular to hear how realistically the sounds were duplicated. If you closed your eyes, you could not distinguish between real and imitation.

LIVE FAST before your clock strikes 12

The flutes sounded like birds. The oboe and kazoo sounded like ducks. The clarinets sounded like cats. The trumpets sound like elephants. The thumb piano sounded like crickets.

There were many other sounds, created by the great variation of other instruments.

You would hear barking, howls, bird songs, growling, meowing, purring, roaring, and braying, a ll created by talented musicians and their well-tuned instruments.

This was always a popular performance, especially for the children. They would join in a recreation of those animals, which sounded like the day of the protest.

There were foods available with animal names. For example: Bombay Duck, Monkey Bread, Tuna Salads, Rabbit Hopping Popcorn, and many more.

The aim of the festival was to highlight humans and animals together. They had consistently been successful.

Dran's family had changed their minds several times about what they would wear. They had gone to the animal sanctuary and spent time looking at the movements of the animals. Mia was observing their skins while considering the difficulty in making costumes for the four of them.

With Dran having such an attachment to bears, he suggested Goldilocks and the three bears. It did not take much convincing. They all thought it was an innovative idea. Dran allowed the boys to choose their character first. When it was all said and done, Mia was Goldilocks, and Dran and the boys were the three bears. Mia did her best to design their costumes, trying to stay true to the characters. They were all pleased with the outcome. Their costumes were not as elaborate as some, but they were pleased with the results. They were proud of the authenticity.

When they arrived at the festival, they were in awe of the large crowd already waiting to come through the gates. Dran assumed his duty station to ensure the count stayed within regulation. Mia and the boys went inside. There were people there from many of the neighboring towns but also from different states. Though they were anxious to come in, they were required to remove the masks enough for their face to show before entering, for the purpose of security.

It was fun to walk around the river and observe the detailed costumes. It was also a funny exercise to guess who was behind the mask when their face was covered. If they did not use their voice, they could keep up the facade for a long time. But once they said something, the voice often gave their identity away.

In addition to the costumes, there were stage performances, storytelling, demonstrations, crafts, and vendors. There were plenty of things to keep you busy for the entire day.

Mia had served as a volunteer at one of the ticket booths, but she had a replacement at 1:00 p.m. This freed her up to enjoy all the afternoon festivities. It was impressive to see that a town the size of Gua could deliver such a first-class festival. It was being broadcast all over the world. Mia had been well entertained and amused for several hours, but now she was ready to go home to rest.

They had been there since 8:00 a.m. The time was now 4:00 p.m., and Mia was very tired. The boys were having so much fun that they did not want to leave. They were tired, but they did not want to miss anything when it came to the animal festival.

It was fine with Mia if the boys stayed with their dad, for she could appreciate the quiet time at home for a few hours before they returned. It would be much less demanding, and she could relax her body and mind.

After getting some rest, she looked forward to drafting a contributive article to submit to the local paper about the event. There was so much to cover that she was certain it would require several articles to address the various aspects of the festival.

Dran could not leave now, because he was also part of the volunteer clean-up crew. He would need to stay until all the grounds were clear. He just had to keep his eyes on the boys. It helped that so many of his cousins were in attendance and they would gladly keep a watchful eye.

There was one of Dran's cousins that lived nearby. She was preparing to head back to her house after finishing a long day at the festival. She offered to give Mia a ride home, since she had to pass by their house to get to her own. It was a convenient solution to this dilemma, and Mia gladly accepted.

Dran was floating all over the festival. He covered a lot of ground as he assisted in making sure everything flowed smoothly. He enjoyed seeing people he had not seen since his early school years. They were catching up on what had happened in their lives over the long timespan. They could not cover nearly as much as they would have loved to, but it was pleasant to reconnect.

The day had been a resounding success and a memorable one. As a representative for the animal reservation, he could not have been more pleased. Dran was pleased to hear that the consensus from the crowds was they could not wait until next year. They were thinking of other people they would bring to share in the festivities. They were also discussing what animal they would dress as the following year. Some were beginning their designs immediately on their return home.

At 5:30 p.m., Dran noticed the crowd was beginning to dwindle. He checked at the gate for the attendance count, and it confirmed that his observations were accurate. This was a wonderful time for him to sit down and take a fifteen-minute break while the rest of the crowd cherished the last hour. He needed to relax his feet and prepare for the big cleaning job ahead.

He verified the location of the boys, who had connected with some of their cousins there. They were riding one of the merry-go-rounds built with all sea animals. They were still having fun.

As he was sitting on a bench, he scanned an aerial view of the grounds and the river. The river was as clear and beautiful as ever. It had the blue, glistening, calm water. He thought of all the animals that lived beneath that huge waterbed. There was an entire world of life out there. It was a perfect backdrop for the celebration.

He recalled going there fishing with his father and his friend Boss. He remembered catching all those fish without any explanation as to where they came from right where he was standing. It was one of the many mysteries of Gua. He had an inner persuasion that someone or something had placed those fish there just for him.

From a distance, he saw a person he thought he recognized. He had seen so many people and so many costumes, he could not be sure. The stance and walk were remarkably familiar.

Dran got up from the bench and walked over by the river toward the person. He called out his name. "Charles, is that you?" There was no answer. He turned his head and walked closer. As they got within several feet of one another, Dran could see his eyes. He knew it was someone he had seen before, but it was not Charles.

He was certainly impressed at the elaborate details of that costume. Dran was still in his Goldilocks bear costume, but he thought the bear costume he was looking at put his costume to shame.

It was at that moment that Dran realized he was looking in the eye of a real bear. There was no costume. Once he realized his current reality, he began to back away slowly. He did not move his eyes from the bear's eyes. They both continued to stare at one another as they both moved backward. When the bear reached the riverbank, he waved his paw and dropped from the two-leg stance to the four-leg crawl. Dran got a good chance to see how massive the bear was. Neither of them uttered a sound.

As soon as Dran broke the stare, the bear turned and ran into the woods.

Dran's legs were feeling weak. He needed to go back and sit on the bench. He realized that he was the only one that knew it was a real bear. He wondered if the bear had been there all day, watching him. He dared not cause a panic by saying something to the remaining crowd. There would be no reason to cause a commotion at this point. There were a few people that were still enjoying the festivities.

The people left the festival that day thinking it was only an elaborate costume. They never dreamed there had been a real live grizzly bear. Dran never mentioned the encounter with anyone.

Dran continued to ponder the mystery as to why the bear was such a tangible part of his life.

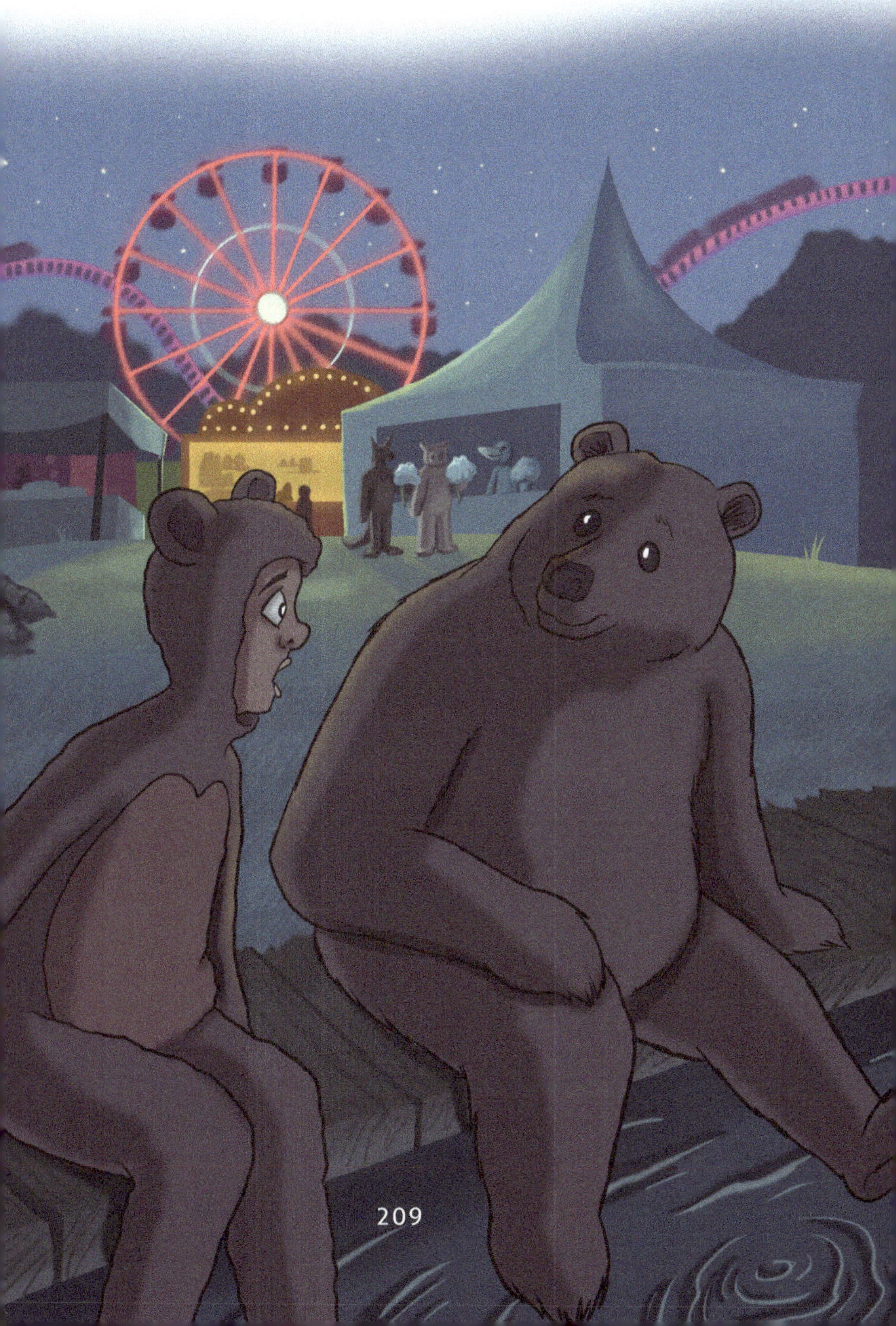

VIVIAN WARD NEWTON

It's 11:59 p.m.

We came here on a mission.

A purpose was at hand.

A bear roaming in the forest,

and a determined and curious man.

But the clock was on a mission

to reach another day.

I did all that I could to keep those little hands at bay.

But I learned that every tick

was measured by design.

The clock fulfilled its purpose

as assigned by our divine.

LIVE FAST *before your clock strikes* **12**

A Time to Reflect and Harvest:
ATTRIBUTES AT 06:00 P.M. TO 11:59 P.M.

This is a reflective time.
It is a time to look back over the last three quarters and start to make sense of
life's mistakes and challenges.
It brings a deep introspection.
Most lives are at a slower pace.
There is the physical and mental culmination of life's journey.
There is a synthesis of intellect and emotions.
There is the desire to impart legacies.
This is a time to share stories, lessons, and love.
It is a time for closure and a time to make peace with one's path.
It is time to understand life's cyclical nature.

LIFE OF REB AND DRAN AT MIDNIGHT

Reb Unites with Dran

Reb had continued to share his knowledge with the younger bears. The time spent with them was one of the more joyous and fulfilling acts of his day. It had proven to be highly effective, and as a result, he developed several extraordinary prodigies. He was optimistic that they were competent torchbearers.

He now had more time to spend with his friend Storm. They would speak of their offspring, which now included a third generation. Reb had fathered two cubs, but Storm had now fathered eight. It was hard to believe that their little ones now had cubs of their own. Where had the time gone?

The truck collision accident years ago had left Storm a little battered. The residue of the incident was a limp in his hind leg and periodic pain. It had not dampened his spirit or hindered his life much. He accepted the pain as a reminder of how fortunate he was to still be alive. He gracefully accepted his limitations and yet continued to thrive. He was particularly grateful for all the encouragement Reb had rendered during his worst time. It was a factual statement to say he did not know what he would have done without him.

They were now at a point where their lives were relived through appreciative conversations. It was wonderful to share their stories with others, but sometimes the stories served as a source for a much-needed chuckle.

Reb and Storm enjoyed life at the animal sanctuary. It was a relief to no longer fear their demise at the hands of humans. When they traveled through the forest, they would often do hunting expeditions and even share the meals. Though bears seldom share food, their long-term friendship inspired the exception.

Living at the sanctuary was now tranquil and peaceful. Reb would often reflect on the journey that brought it to this point. This newfound state had changed the landscape and mindscape for the better in all of Gua.

The importance of communication between the animals and humans stood out as the most significant factor in the turnaround. There were many species of animals and humans from all levels of society willing to avail themselves for compromise.

The resourcefulness from nonverbal forest animals was the greatest performance of a desperate act to ensure survival. Their chances of prevailing were extremely low. But their feeling of despair reverted to an elaborate display of courage.

He had done many impactful things in his life, but he was most proud of the way the animal protest had inspired other causes around the world. They would find ways to effectively communicate their grievances. With mutual respect, change would be inevitable.

Reb's life had been a lifestyle of excitement, limited extravagance, and practical risk-taking. He was motivated by an urgency to get things done. He always felt he was on a mission much bigger than himself. His greatest cause was to help humanity and leave the world better than when he arrived. He felt a sense of accomplishment in one particular area of his life.

Reb had been withholding a lifelong secret. There had been occurrences in his life that he had never shared with a single soul. Though he and Storm were best friends, and they shared most events in their lives, he had not been at liberty to share these events with him. But now, he deemed it was time to reveal some of the withheld mysteries. There was no one he trusted any more than Storm. They had been one another's greatest confidants over the years.

One afternoon after sharing a meal, Reb casually mentioned that he would like to talk with him the next day. Storm felt nothing suspicious about that request. They had had many talks before. He agreed to the meeting, bade farewell, then retired for the evening for a good night's sleep.

Reb, on the other hand, was deeply unsettled. He tossed and turned, getting truly little sleep. Dawn lingered, but after a long night, Reb finally saw the sun break through. He paced back and forth all day, waiting for their time to talk.

Reb had always been comfortable at the tree where so many gatherings happened. This is where, once again, they would meet. The clock eventually brought them to the planned time.

Reb did not really know where to begin, so he started by saying he hoped this information would not change their friendship. He did not think it would, but that was an opening icebreaker. He then began his confession.

On the day that he was born, there was a human boy named Dran born at the exact same time in the town of Gua. They traveled together to earth, and only one mile's distance separated their arrival.

Unexplainable things happened in Gua with the weather at both births. There was snow, warmth, storms, and ice all confined within the one-mile radius of their births. The circumstances surrounding both births were laced with uncommon occurrences. It was something never seen before and had never been seen again. The town's residents still talked about it till now.

From day one, Reb knew he would have a special companion that was totally different from him. They would have very few similarities, but he was to assist and protect whenever and wherever their paths crossed.

He had accompanied him during many phases of his life. Most of them, Dran never knew he was there.

He knew of Dran's stuffed animal named Benno and all the joy it had given him. It had served as a constant reminder that the bear was his lasting companion.

He remembered the first time he and Dran had seen one another. It was on the school trip to the animal reserve. Reb had been there waiting for him to arrive. Due to their inability to communicate, he could not tell him who he was. He endeavored to show his affection through his playfulness. At least Reb knew that Dran liked him.

He had been the one to leave the fish for Dran at the river. Dran almost caught him placing them there, but he escaped by only a couple of minutes.

The summer school performance had been very absorbing to him. He had watched the entire production from the edge of the woods. But there had been a gross misunderstanding. Dran thought he had taken the jacket. It was quite the contrary. His two bear friends had snatched the jacket from the door. When Dran saw them with the clothing on the ground, Reb was attempting to get the jacket from his friends. He wanted to return it. He had wished he could explain that to Dran, but he could only smile and wink to get the message across.

At the strawberry patch with Dran's cousins, Reb had cleared the patch before they arrived. He wanted to make it easy for Dran.

Had he come alone, he would have left several pails of strawberries waiting for him as he had done with the fish years ago. In addition, he wanted him to enjoy the picking experience with his cousins. He knew that Dran would be alone when he came back to the tree to retrieve the stick. That was why Reb showed himself in the tree. He communicated how much he cared for his well-being.

Reb could not miss the celebration at the river. That was reminiscent of the animal protest. The memories of that day resonated deeply within Reb. He made his presence known to Dran when the crowd dwindled. He was telling Dran that he appreciated all he had done to help the Gua animals. His contributions would long be felt throughout the forest.

When he stared at Dran in his eyes, he always hoped that the saying he had often heard was true. It says, "The eyes are the windows of the soul." When the eyes of the two interlocked together during each encounter, the hope was that it would reveal a lot about the inner feelings and emotions.

Dran had many suspicions over the years, but he had not understood the dynamics the two of them shared.

Reb had now spilled all these mysteries to his dear friend. It felt good to finally get this off his chest. He felt immensely relieved. He had come close to sharing these details with Storm before, but the timing never seemed to feel right. This opportune moment had brought them to the place of perfect timing.

It would not change the relationship as friends nor Reb's commitment to continue doing what he had always done. He knew his secrets were safe with Storm. It would forever remain their secret.

These had been some of the most bizarre revelations Storm had ever heard. As he thought about it, things started to make sense. The entire animal community knew from his birth that there was something vastly different about Reb. However, they would never guess that it was to this monstrous extent.

Reb thanked Storm for listening, and they parted ways.

When Reb returned to the animal sanctuary, he could not calm his mind enough to go to sleep. He paced back and forth until finally he realized sleep was evading him. He considered several options, one of which was to summon Storm again for more talking. Instead, he decided to roam through the familiar grounds of the forest. He had been on this path many times before. He knew it so well that he could maneuver it with his eyes closed.

Over the years, he had found the nights were his best time to wander. It was also a time to keep his body active, both physically and mentally. He liked being out there, mostly alone. Occasionally he would see other animals foraging, but that was not very often.

Since Dran lived nearby, he would frequent the residential area to surveil things. It was a way to make sure Dran was OK.

Since he could not sleep, this would be a wonderful time to check in on him.

One of the greatest advantages of maneuvering at night was that no one witnessed what he was doing. Over the previous weeks, he had been seen by Dran's family dog even though he attempted to remain inconspicuous. He would try hard to be extremely careful.

The night was a great one for roaming. It was a warm summer night. Once he began walking, the weather began to get cooler. The more he walked, the colder it became. Pretty soon, the temperature was freezing. It was perplexing, because the sky seemed divided into two parts. The weather change of cold was confined between the area of the sanctuary and Dran's house. The rest of the sky was consistent with a typical summer night. It was vibrant with a few soft clouds. There was mostly an ocean of twinkling stars.

Reb trekked his way through the arctic-type cold. His thick layer of blubber and the denseness of his two layers of fur had never failed to keep him warm before now. He hoped to get through this territory within a few minutes. He could see in the sky that the weather was warm not far away.

Reb's teeth were chattering. He started to tremble. The only time he remembered that happening was on the day he was born. He had experienced traveling down the tunnel cold and wet until he made it through his mom's womb. It seemed he was experiencing nostalgic recalls. He made his way to within steps of Dran's yard. The weather was still cold, but he was getting remarkably close to the warm weather change.

Reb could see a human figure standing in the front yard. It was Dran. He began to walk toward him at a methodical pace. He realized that Dran had seen him also. He could see the strides that Dran was making toward him. They soon came to a one-on-one meeting. When they met in the front yard, they stopped and stared into each other's eyes.

The trembles from Reb completely stopped, and his body immediately reached a cozy summer night's temperature. He was definitely not cold anymore; rather, he felt a sweltering rush of heat. This was yet another unexplainable mystery in Gua.

Everything in him wanted to give Dran a big bear hug. He refrained, and instead he stood on two legs, reached out his paw, and placed it in Dran's hands. They exchanged smiles.

The soft clouds overhead multiplied and continued to dance in the sky, forming scenes of people and animals. It was an eloquent conglomeration of diversity. Reb and Dran watched as if they were viewing a movie. The bear that Dran's father had seen in the clouds was once again a profound figure, continually widening.

When the sky display ceased, the starlight twinkled from the effects of the wind and air. The different temperatures and densities contributed to the brilliant exhibit.

LIVE FAST *before your clock strikes* **12**

They did not try to communicate. They did not need to. It was all done from the heart. Again, they smiled at one another and finally embraced in the long-awaited big bear hug. They both had one to offer. Then they interlocked hand in hand and began to walk toward downtown Gua. After a few steps of walking, the sky lit up with fireworks in downtown Gua, and for the first time in forty years, the majestic clock struck twelve midnight.

Dran Unites with Reb

Dran had a wonderful time at the animal festival celebration. The experience of gathering with friends and family reminded him of the reason he moved back to Gua. He had no regrets about his decision. Neither did Mia. He felt especially secure that his Gua relatives would always be supportive of him and his family. They enjoyed spending time together, but his family also respected his time and space. This arrangement worked because it was one of mutual respect.

Dran and Mia had quickly become accustomed to their different environment. The home that they purchased was in a terrific location with several acres. There was lots of space for the boys inside and out.

They loved their new school, which happened to be the same one that Dran had attended. Part of the school looked the same, but there had been dramatic updated renovations.

The competitive nature of the boys made them outstanding stars on the school's sports team. Their skills surpassed Dran's sports history, but he could not be prouder. He and Mia supported the teams financially and with their frequent attendance at the school's sports games.

The opportunity for his boys to grow up with their cousins was invaluable. Together they participated in many of the family traditions that stemmed back to Dran's childhood. There was such a sense of pride watching the boys interacting with their cousins, just as he had done when he was their age.

Both Dran and Mia had quickly become hometown celebrities. Their careers were excelling. Dran had unexpectedly become a political enthusiast after he had been so successful in governing the animal sanctuary. He enjoyed it so much that he did not consider it work but instead a privilege. Though there were many other areas of his life, he could never get away from his passion for animals.

It coincided with the ownership of his father's veterinarian business. After his father's retirement, Dran took over control of the facility. He was not involved in the day-to-day operation of the business; instead, he hired a full staff to take care of all the animals' needs. He did, however, continue to make sure everything ran smoothly.

In addition to his already-busy schedule, he would still do scheduled performances at many local events. He was still a sought-after entertainer because he was known to bring in sell-out crowds.

Mia was a skillful reporter. She was never short of interesting articles to submit to the local news outlets. She was a coveted journalist because of her dependability for truth and insightful knowledge.

Even with all the current changes and their extremely busy schedule, they were content with the state of their lives.

With their many demands, they still found time to travel. They took the boys to several sites in and out of the country for some unforgettable trips.

Some of their favorite trips were the ones they made back to Atsu. It was important and fulfilling to spend time with Mia's family. It was always a joy to reconnect with people he had met while he lived there. He would frequently see his friend that made his Atsu stay possible.

When they were there for a weekend, he would stop in and do a couple of sets at Notes & Jokes. It was especially rewarding to see the second location flourishing. Whichever place he performed, he would still leave the patrons wanting him to stick around longer. It was great to still be appreciated, but they valued having the best of both worlds.

He had sentimental thoughts about his many friends and their unwavering devotion to one another. None of their lives had been perfect, but it had been good and full of variations. They supported each other through thick and thin. He honored them as true treasures.

When Dran reflected on various times during his entire existence, he thought of the many experiences he'd had in his forty years. He had been able to squeeze in many adventures within this brief period. He managed to live life at a rapid pace, but he left enough footprints in the paths to make a difference for himself and many others.

There had been many incidents where the positive results had no logical explanations. There were things that defied the odds for successful outcomes, but he somehow managed to persevere.

One of the things that had remained a lingering perplexity was the association he had with the grizzly bears. It stayed at the forefront of his mind as to why the several bear encounters occurred at different intervals in his life. He pondered over these incidents often.

From the time he was a child, a bear had continued to appear in different decades of his life. He even thought about his attachment to Benno, his stuffed bear friend and companion. There was always an unexplainable comfort when Benno was close by. He needed to see him the last thing at night and the first thing in the morning for his day to have a good start.

He had been presented with many other toys over the years, but none of them could override his loyalty to Benno. Why was it one of his first toys as a baby? Was this all just a part of his vivid imagination? He wondered if he was the only person in Gua experiencing these bizarre happenings.

Though he had these thoughts, he never felt comfortable discussing them with anyone. He did not want to sound weird. There were many documented mysteries in Gua, but this was something that affected him personally, which made all the difference.

He remembered how one of his worst days ever was when he lost Benno at the school show-n-tell. He had been in such a state of panic he could barely breathe. There could not be any imagination strong enough to see his life without him. That was a traumatic time for him, and he believed it was to Benno. There was undoubtedly something magical about that toy. He was definitely not an ordinary stuffed animal.

He began to chronicle different encounters that had reoccurred in his forty years. He remembered his school bus ride to the animal reserve. The young cub took special interest in him and followed him as long as he was in sight. He remembered even giving him a name. Something about naming him made it feel personal enough that they were friends. Even one of the reserve workers said he had never seen anything like that before. Everyone who witnessed the encounter agreed that it was an extremely strange engagement.

On the day that he, his father, and Boss went fishing, he believed that the fish waiting for him had been placed there. He never saw a bear, but he had the suspicion that the bear had gifted him with the school of fish.

Then there was the theater incident at summer camp. The missing-coat saga had been one of the greatest adrenaline rushes ever to him. He never dreamed he would experience a face-to-face confrontation with a bear. The bigger surprise was witnessing the return of the jacket without any injuries to it, himself, or the bear.

There was the bear from the strawberry patch. Dran felt that the bear had watched him the entire time. He obviously meant no harm to anyone in the group, but he was curious as to why he was there. Their hands had actually touched one another, but there had been no fear. It was more like a touch of friendship.

The most recent one was the animal festival at the river. This had to be more than a coincidence. Out of all the thousands of people in attendance, he was the only person that realized he was staring in the eyes of a real grizzly bear.

Dran was convinced that there had been many other times that the bear was around him but was not identified. He often felt a presence, as if someone was watching him. It was not paranoia or a delusional belief, even though other people might beg to differ.

What did the bears mean to him? What had he been trying to tell him all these years? He was not worried or afraid. He was earnestly puzzled.

Dran had long accepted that Gua was a mysterious place. From the day of his birth until now, he had unexplainable things happen to him.

There were people who had watched him grow up, who reminded him of the mysteries of his birth. They had always believed he was exceptional. Graciously, they would share how proud they were to see him so focused on carrying out what he embraced as his life's purpose.

Dran could not tie all his life together to make cohesive sense, but he could only hope that he had carried out what he should have up until this point in time. What he could acknowledge was that he had tried to remain true to himself.

Dran and Mia took immense pleasure in living near the animal reserve. When the house was quiet at night, they could hear the sounds of nature. He would equate it to living close to a rainforest.

Their dog equally enjoyed the serene atmosphere. He would sometimes lie out on the porch and sleep to the engaging, soothing sounds. He enjoyed spending as much time outside as he did inside.

The dog had been a great playmate for the boys. They had learned the responsibilities of having a pet while respecting the life of another creature. They considered him a part of their family. It was predicted that they would carry on the animal-care legacy that had been in their family for generations.

After the dog had been with them a few months, he established his routine. He would make his usual morning run, chasing the birds. This routine had become a part of his daily exercise. They estimated he usually ran around about five miles per day. He would run around the yard and up and down the pathway to the fence. His routine had become predictable, so it was quite noticeable when he deviated from the norm.

The dog had started to act very strangely over a two-day period. He stayed remarkably close to the front steps of the porch. Periodically, he would raise his head, look around, and lay his head down again. This was not characteristic of the dog at all.

They checked each of his paws to make sure there was not an injury. They also checked for splinters stuck in his paw that would prevent his usual activities. There was not a noticeable cause for discomfort.

It puzzled them for a few days. Then they made the decision to take him to the veterinarian's office for a thorough examination. The examination further showed no injury.

When they returned from the veterinarian, they noticed the dog kept looking down by the edge of the woods. When he lay on the porch, he would raise his head at an angle, taking a quick glance in the same area of the yard. They wanted to get to the root cause of this unusual behavior.

LIVE FAST before your clock strikes 12

Early one morning, one of the boys ran down the hallway. He was so excited that his words could barely flow from his mouth. There were stutters, "huh"s, and even some silence in a span of about two minutes.

Finally, he stuttered, "There is a bear outside. He is down by the edge of the fence."

Now, it all made sense. That was what was wrong with the dog. He had seen the bear all along. He was frightened and would not go anywhere near the fence. The mystery was solved.

They were not as fearful for themselves as they were for the dog. Leaving the dog in the yard could potentially be dangerous to him.

The bear was not anywhere near them, but they all tiptoed down the hall like he was. They peeped from the window down near the fence where the bear was sighted. They were about a half football field from one another.

From that distance, they could see the shadow of a creature much larger than a human. There was a slight motion, and they could see about one-fourth of his body.

They could see his huge, hairy body. He was the largest bear any of them had ever seen, except for Dran. He quickly came to the conclusion that this was the bear he had seen at the celebration. He was all too familiar.

Dran reminded the boys that they would not in any way cause harm to the bear, because they were not being threatened. He also reminded the boys of the ordinances that were in place in Gua, and they would adhere to them.

He thought that the bear must have gotten off the path and needed to find his way back to the animal sanctuary not too far away.

The more Dran stared, the more certain he was that he was experiencing another bear encounter. Dran thought again of the previous bear encounters he had in the past. It was the school trip, at the mountain theater, the strawberry patch, at the animal protest celebration and now this encounter at his house.

As Dran thought about all of this, he thought of another encounter he missed. The bear was the same one he had seen on television leading the animal protest. He could not mistake those eyes.

The bear's size had changed and grown over time, but so had Dran's. The thing that remained consistent was the eyes. There was always a sincerity he witnessed while looking in his face. It was as if they knew one another.

Could this be the same bear? Had the bear followed him his entire life? This whole thought process seemed impossible, but how could it be explained?

The topic of discussion the rest of the evening was, of course, the bear. Mia suggested contacting the animal sanctuary round-up officials on Monday to see if they could entice the bear to inhabit the residence with the other bears.

Up until now, Dran had not shared any of the encounters. But now, he felt compelled to be honest with his family. This was the first time the bear had affected his family directly. Dran shared the many encounters he experienced over the years from the time he was a little boy. He even told them about receiving Benno, his stuffed bear, when he was a baby.

They had known of Dran's attachment to Benno, even as an adult. The boys had seen him but had never been able to play with him. They knew he was special, from their dad's childhood.

The stories were fascinating but confusing to Dran's family. They wondered if this was something they would all experience as they continued to grow up in Gua. Would the bear continue to associate with Dran's family?

They stayed up all night discussing the shocking situation with the bear. Every day after then, they would all look down by the fence for the bear to emerge.

Three days passed, and they had not seen the bear. Even the dog was more comfortable roaming in the yard. Hopefully, he had found his way to the sanctuary.

Dran's thoughts on the bear situation had become more intense. He did not know how the revelation would affect his family or if they would begin to experience similar encounters.

When they all went to bed, Dran could not sleep. He did not want to wake anyone, so he walked out onto the porch and then into the yard. He looked around to see if he was alone. He pivoted a complete 360 degrees. He searched from all the angles. Nothing looked strange or seemed out of place. It was reassuring to not see anything, yet he was disappointed that he still had no answers.

Dran had gotten the fresh air, so now he figured that would help him get the sleep he craved. As he climbed the porch stairs, he made a final glance toward the fence. In the shadow from the moon, there stood the big bear. Dran stood still. Should he go, or should he run back inside?

He stepped off the porch and back into the yard. He began moving closer to the bear. Strangely, the bear moved closer to him. When they reached the middle of the yard, they both stopped and stared at one another. Dran knew it had been the same bear all along. He had followed him throughout his life. The eyes interlocked, and they both smiled.

The soft clouds in the sky began to multiply, and there were vivid scenes of people and animals. Dran and Reb stood there watching as if they were at a movie. They both embraced one another and offered up the biggest bear hug ever.

The bear stood on two legs. He extended his paw out to interlock Dran's arm. They touched each other and, hand in hand, they began to walk together toward downtown Gua.

In the distance, the sky was illuminated. Among the brilliance of the light, Dran and Reb could hear the downtown clock bellowing out a big *bong*, and the clock, for the first time in forty years, struck midnight.

BONG!

LIVE FAST *before your clock strikes* 12

It's Midnight

Well, it is now midnight.

We tried to get it all in.

I am glad to report on our successes.

Promotions: king bear and king men.

VIVIAN WARD NEWTON

The tunnel that brought us in this world
took us back to where we began.
We learned in this life's journey,
it was all part of a plan.
Our message to those that are listening to the sound of the ticking clock:
just know that each sound you hear brings
you closer to your earthly disembark.
Live fast and with intention,
and do it with all your might;
leave nothing undone or unfinished
before your clock strikes midnight.

LIVE FAST *before your clock strikes* 12

A Time of Reward: Attributes at Midnight

Midnight is a symbol of transition.
Midnight marks the end of each day in
time throughout the world.
It is a sixty-second moment that separates one day from the next.
It often declares the long night is over.
It is the threshold between yesterday's triumphs
or failures and tomorrow's possibilities.
It is often symbolically used to describe a major change in our life's experiences.
The culmination at midnight reflects the beautiful complexity of the human experience.
By recognizing these moments of time, individuals can cultivate resilience,
embrace change, and find contentment during each day.
Each day offers unique lessons and experiences, reminding everyone of the
shared journey through these universal time reckonings.

John 17:4

APPENDIX: IT HELPS TO KNOW

The Significance of the Number Twelve

The number twelve is used throughout our culture and that of many ancient cultures worldwide. It has been considered a mysterious number in that there were those that believed that this two-digit number had a special meaning. It stood out with particular importance in history and religion. In general, it represented perfection, entirety, or cosmic order in traditions since early history.

In ancient times, there was a fascination that led to people developing an entire numerical system separate from mathematics.

This number was considered by some to be sacred. It is believed that this title was derived from the ancient "dozen system," which was a unique numbering system in the Neolithic era. This was the "New Stone Age," a final division of the Stone Age in Europe, Asia, and Africa. After this time, the bronze material began to replace the stone, which eventually phased out the Stone Age entirely.

Religious and Cultural Significance of Twelve

- Christianity—twelve Apostles of Jesus, twelve tribes of Israel
- Judaism—twelve sons of Jacob, twelve months in the Hebrew lunar calendar
- Islam—twelve imams revered in Shi'ite Islam
- Hinduism—twelve Jyotirlinga shrines—sacred temples honoring Shiva
- Buddhism—twelve links in the Buddhist concept of dependent origination
- Ancient Egypt—twelve stages of passing into the afterlife
- Chinese Zodiac—twelve-year cycle, with each year named after an animal

The spiritual symbolism of twelve crosses cultural boundaries, suggesting an innate mystical quality. "Religions likely integrated the significance of twelve because it resonated with ancient beliefs in its cosmic depth" (http://www.33rdsquare.com).

In practically all cultures, twelve represents completeness and divine order. The pattern continues in modern everyday life. It is incorporated in measurements, music, and mythology. They all reinforce the significance of the number twelve.

The number twelve has stood the test of time and carried us through many centuries of practical application.

In any country, regardless of their time system, midnight starts a new day. Midnight is known as the most momentous time for revelation and dreams.

It is denoted as a peaceful ending of day. It brings us to a pivotal point. Midnight is a combination of the words *mid* (morning) and *niht* (night). It is the transition from one day to the next.

Midnight carries a strong level of mystery. It has produced many folklores and credence surrounding the mystique this number brings. There are some who believe midnight is the darkest part of the night. It has been labeled as a time when the veil is the thinnest in the spiritual realm. It is shrouded with the eeriness of teetering between the known and the unknown. It hovers between the conscious and the unconscious. Midnight is considered a time of reflection and contemplation. Because the mind is thought to be relaxed and open, people are thought to often be faced with pivotal decisions. There is a reverence about midnight. Things often happen that are often unexplainable and baffle your mind. Many cultures conduct rituals at this chosen time.

There have been movies written about midnight. They have intrigued audiences with the lure of uncertainty. The movie *Cinderella* depicts a total transformation at midnight. It is an example

LIVE FAST *before your clock strikes* **12**

of things changing back to the way they were previously when the clock strikes the bewitching hour.

With these examples, you will see how the number twelve continues to play such a vital role in our everyday lives:

- Number of hours on a clock
- Number twelve carries religious, mythological, and magical symbols
- Number represents perfection
- Number represents entirety
- Number often used in the context of government
- A composite number divisible by two, three, four, and six
- The largest number with one syllable
- Number of months in a year
- Number of hours in a day
- Number of hours in a night
- Number of signs in the zodiac
- Number of stations of the moon and sun
- Number of members on a jury
- Number of eggs in a dozen
- Number of things to be called a duodecad
- Number of ribs on the average human
- Number of inches in a foot
- Number of days of Christmas
- Number of face cards in a deck
- Number of strikes in a perfect bowling game

- Number of basic hues on the color wheel
- Number of blood weight in our body (1/12)
- Number appears 187 times throughout the Old/New Testament
- Number in the Bible associated with perfection of order and government
- Number of spies scouting the Promise Land
- Number of fruits in Revelation, Tree of Life
- Number of Jacob's sons
- Number of Jesus's disciples
- Number of the tribes of Israel
- Number of the age Jesus's ministry began
- Number of kinds of fruit in the tree of life
- Number of stars in the US flag
- Number of alphabets in Hawaiian alphabets
- Number of animal signs in the Chinese zodiac
- Number of Olympians in Greek mythology
- Number of notes in a chromatic musical scale
- Number of pitch classes in Western tonal music

In the story *Live Fast before Your Clock Strikes Twelve*, Reb and Dran begin a life where seconds, minutes, hours, weeks, and months become years. Their clocks are ticking at the exact same time. They shared the rotation of the sun each day. The curiosity surrounding the oddity of their coexistence is whimsical and

LIVE FAST before your clock strikes 12

yet quite solemn. The perplexing relationship throughout their lives leaves you in an enchanted frame of mind. Life has not been a rehearsal but a real-life performance. They both participate in thrilling acts and dramatic roles. There is not a written script but minute-by-minute impromptu routines. Midnight brings about their final curtain call.

At midnight in the city of Gua, the downtown clock strikes again after forty years. It is a sound they missed yet hoped to hear again. They understand clearly that the mystery of it all is the charm that makes the city so eccentric and desirable.

As the clock gives off the long-awaited *bong*, Reb and Dran accept that the bell is tolling for both. They embrace one another so closely that they are like one, and they slip into obscurity on the other side of midnight. Dran and Reb are together again.

What has the story shown us? The hypothetical scenario could suggest it was a dream or a symbol designed to trigger the evaluation of our lives. It prompts the quest to fill our life's mission and time with determination.

A more pragmatic approach is to accept that these things happened as written and the two lived an entangled, enigmatic life.

In the essay "For Whom the Bell Tolls" by John Donne, he answers that question by acknowledging that because none of us stands alone in the world, each human death affects all of us.

"A Clear Midnight" by *Walt Whitman*
This is thy hour O Soul, thy free flight into the wordless,
Away from books, away from art, the day erased, the lesson done,
Thee fully forth emerging silent, gazing, pondering the themes thou lovest best,
Night, sleep, death, and the stars.

The Significance of Life

The symbolism of Reb and Dran is meant to give an insightful perspective on what could happen with two unlikely creatures living remarkably similar lives.

The story presents the possibility of these two lives eventually not only gaining tolerance but reaching mutual respect. The obvious diversity between the two is the catalyst for change to benefit them both. In a world where differences are continually emphasized, there are incentives to redirect the focus for harmonious relationships. The incentives provide us with comfort; they boost our emotional health and give us a sense of belonging.

But for those that are willing, there are creative ways to make the most out of life. Despite differences in communication styles, differences in values, past conflict, or stubbornness, it is possible to increase our range of knowledge. We sell ourselves short when we refuse to open our heart and mind to possibilities. We share the planet but do not own this planet. All our stays on this earth are temporary.

Are their lives vastly different beyond the obvious of being two distinct species?

Do they have the same needs and desires in life? Can either of them ever define their life's purpose for the time they have on planet earth?

Perhaps the significance of life is relevant to all living creatures.

Perhaps there is no singular meaning of life to stand for us all. We may all have different paths to fulfill our greatest potential and our predestined assignments.

Their similarities run the gamut of probabilities, encompassing environments, relationships, foods, clothing, and shelter. They breathe the same air, often eat the same food, rear a family, socialize in the community, establish relationships, and experience many of the same emotions.

This debate has for years been a subject in some very heated discussions. Everyone wants to believe their life has significant value. They shudder to think that their entire time on planet earth was meaningless. The hope is that their living was not in vain.

This is definitely true for Reb and Dran. Living in a beautiful city called Gua brings them both joy. They did not have a clue that they were born a few miles from each other. On that same day in February, Reb and Dran entered the earth realm from a tunnel of protection through their mothers. They did not know the connection that would later unfold during their lifetime. They discover that there are things and people whose destinies are unknowingly tied to one another.

They both mull over the questions, "Why am I here?" and, "What is the meaning of life?"

They do not have an unequivocal answer. But there is, however, an obvious response—that being the necessity to survive. Without life itself, there is no other thing you can contribute.

What am I surviving to do?

The compatible search for the meaning and significance of life taps into many unlikely resources for Reb and Dran. They encounter many experiences in their pursuit.

For instance, Reb ventures into the forest, requiring him to be a step ahead of the predator.

Further, Dran's life ventures require quick decision-making skills to maneuver through life unscathed.

If Reb and Dran explored the different philosophies of our time, they would come across many schools of thought to this question. It has consumed the minds of many people from all levels of society.

There are many religious and cultural beliefs, many of which have developed their own philosophy.

There are those who find their meaning in personal growth. They strive to learn and do as much as possible to expand their knowledge and increase their awareness. Some would focus on contributing to society, helping their fellow men. This compassionate act, for many, is satisfying and purposeful. Some focus on their connection to another individual as a partnership to go through life together. Then there are those who believe their purpose is based on a spiritual belief. They strive to follow a pathway that is designed by someone greater than themselves.

The beauty of all the schools of thought is that it allows us to connect with our deeper self-search and discover greater revelations about ourselves and others.

There is nothing that we have in life that is permanent. Everything we have, including life itself, is temporary. There will be happy and sad occasions, but even those events will pass. There will be failures and successes, but those too are temporary. In all these cases, there is something to gain from the experience. All failure builds experience, and experience builds growth; growth makes you stronger, and getting stronger produces success.

One of the Christian questions are presented in thoughts to ponder. "We are born in the world without knowing exactly who we are (identity), where we come from (origin), why we are here (meaning), what to live for and how we should live (purpose), and where we are going (destiny).

Many are searching for happiness. There is a distinct difference between finding happiness and finding meaning in life. Seeking happiness does not mean you are living a purposeful life. Seeking meaning and purpose does not mean it will be easy, carefree, or happy.

During the limited time, there are opportunities to learn more about themselves and the people, things, and situations they confront daily.

As Reb and Dran show us, discovering who you are allows you to operate in confidence to complete your assignments. There is no time to linger. The clock is ticking, and the purpose is waiting to be fulfilled.

The uncertainty of our midnight is what makes life so precious. No one knows the fleeting hour for death, but we know of its inevitable arrival. Therefore, we live life to the fullest. As we experience and enjoy, we are reminded that life has significance. Our individual lives are meaningful. We are a part of a greater whole.

When the clock strikes midnight, Reb and Dran both experience an epiphany. They have clarity and insight into what makes life more meaningful. Their reflection of their life shines a light on the things they were able to accomplish. Their limited space and time are altered because they lived.

With their assignment complete, on the other side of midnight, Reb and Dran can walk hand in hand and experience the dawning of a new day.

LIVE FAST before your clock strikes 12

The Significance of Time

Time is one of the most important things in the world. It is fundamental to an existence of any organized consistency. Can you imagine how we would wander through life if we did not have the measurement of time? We could not make our appointments. We could not schedule activities or meetings. There would not be a heartbeat measurement of beats per minute. We would not even know if it were day or night. Time is a way we reference change. It is a basic and necessary component of all our lives. We are dependent on the measurements of time to measure temperature, weight, distance, height, volume, and speed.

We celebrate birthdays, anniversaries, holidays, and other significant days in our lives through time.

Time is something unretrievable. Once it has passed, we cannot get it back. We do not possess the ability to speed time up or to slow time down. It has been said that time carries more value than money, because you have the power to earn what was spent, but you cannot get the time back it took you to earn it.

The breakdown in segments of time includes the units of seconds, minutes, hours, days, weeks, months, years, and centuries. We use these units based on the span we are attempting to measure. Our current instruments used to measure time are the winding clock, electric clock, stopwatch, and the pendulum clock. In the past, the sundial, the water clock, the atomic clock, incense clocks, candle clocks, and hourglasses were frequently used.

A calendar is a modern way to measure times of year, days, and dates. These methods have proven to be an amenity to everyday life.

"Scientists have measured the shortest unit of time ever: the time it takes a light particle to cross a hydrogen molecule. That time, for the record, is 247 zeptoseconds. A zeptosecond is a trillionth of a billionth of a second, or a decimal point followed by twenty zeros and a 1" (Quora.com).

"The largest unit of time is the supereon, composed of eons. Eons are divided into eras, which are in turn divided into periods, epochs, and ages" (wikipedia.org).

Time is continuous. It does not start and stop randomly in our world. It does not require individual activity for it to exist. Time just is. Yet time is subjective.

Albert Einstein's general theory of relativity predicted that gravity and speed influence time; the faster you travel, the more time slows down.

It is not the same everywhere at the same time. It is dependent on speed and gravity. Where gravity is stronger, time is slower.

Think of the different time zones in the world. "Different continents have different time zones due to the Earth's rotation and the way time is measured. Time zones are based on the position of the sun in the sky at a given location. As the Earth rotates, various parts of the planet experience daylight and darkness at contrasting times" (Quora.com).

LIVE FAST *before your clock strikes* **12**

There are some notable quotes that address the importance of time:

"Time is what we want most, but what we use worst" (William Penn).

"Time isn't the main thing. It's the only thing" (Miles Davis).

"A man who dares to waste one hour of time has not discovered the value of life" (Charles Darwin).

"The bad news is time flies; the good news is you're the pilot" (Michael Altshuler).

"Regret for wasted time is more wasted time" (Mason Cooley).

"Your time is limited, so don't waste it living someone else's life" (Steve Jobs).

When we speak of time, we apply it to the various stages of the time duration we have in our lives. We experience changes from our birth to our death. It is a common cliche to say that time brings about change.

There have been examples of stages of life measured using different frames of reference.

These are some forms of life's measurements: They are divided into four stages:

- Seasons of beginning, seasons of full-bloom, seasons of transformation, seasons of reflection
- Seasons of spring, seasons of summer, seasons of fall, seasons of winter

- Stages of dreamer, stages of exploration, stages of builder, stages of mentor/giver
- Stages of introduction, stages of growth, stages of maturity, stages of decline

Each stage covers an age range. Within the range, most people share things in common.

We generally have common interests, behaviors, and similar maturity levels. We experience drastic changes as time progresses in our lives. From birth to death, there is development where we learn and grow.

There are many biological changes that occur during the life cycle and many changes of social impacts. As we develop, we set values, different interests, and some aspirations.

This book divides the stages of life into four chronicles of time. They are in infancy/childhood, adolescence, adulthood, and senior years. It covers the lifespan of Reb and Dran.

From birth, their time brings about many life changes. Not only do they grow physically, but they also grow mentally, spiritually, emotionally, and socially. In a timespan, each life experience brings about specific changes and insightful observations.

Each segment of their time is an area of self-discovery.

Infancy/childhood is an exciting time for both of their parents. They both are dependent on their parents for nourishment and guidance. Through observation, they mimic their behavior, thus learning to walk and talk. The life lessons being learned are the stepping stone to the next stage of their lives. They were trusting of their surroundings and their significant role in society would play.

Adolescence is an equally exciting time but with less dependence. They are becoming more responsible for their actions, yet they both have the support of their parents and surroundings. They are excused for many of their mistakes. They test their boundaries. They are both at a point of learning. Their major contribution to society is their willingness to explore and experiment.

Adulthood is a time of becoming more independent. They become grounded in their personal successes and in their place in the community. They are both self-sufficient and quite established. They are both contributors in society and respected in the community. Their major contribution is that of contributing.

As seniors, they are interdependent. They both have people in their lives where they could support one another. They are accepting of the role of mentorship and passing on any wisdom that they have. They are enjoying the relationships that have been established. They are more in a stage of relaxing. Their major bequest is mentoring and benevolence.

Dran and Reb's lives have significantly close parallels.

The Significance of the Tree

Throughout history, there has always been a place to gather to bring your thoughts and ideas. The tree is deeply rooted in the earth and is an inspiration and embodiment of a sturdy foundation. Yet trees flex and sway with the wind when needed.

We look to the tree for medicinal healing as well as spiritual healing. We grace our homes, gardens, and sacred grounds as a reminder that there is someone greater than ourselves.

Humans and trees have similar physical characteristics. We stand upright and have a crown and limbs stemming from a central trunk.

A tree has filled this role in many neighborhoods throughout our society. The tree contributes to the environment by providing oxygen, improving air quality, conserving water, and preserving soil.

The tree supports numerous living creatures. It accommodates everyone from the largest mammal to the tiniest creatures. They travel in the deepest crevices to the highest branches to the fragile leaves and the woody bark.

The animals living in the tree (arboreal animals) adapt to benefit the most from their leafy surroundings. Some examples are sloths, opossums, geckos, spider monkeys, and tree kangaroos.

Many other animals use the tree for resting, nesting, and a place to capture their prey.

Birds nest in branches, baboons devour the fruit, bats drink nectar, and elephants consume parts of the entire tree.

There, the animals can drink from the tree trunk. They can share knowledge, hear suggestions, and strategize their next step.

In the Disney movie *The Lion King*, the baobab tree is Rafiki's home. There also is the tree in *Avatar* (The Tree of Souls) and the *Madagascar* movie.

In addition to meeting the needs of the animal kingdom, it plays a vital part in the lives of humans. The tree has served as a place of rest and meditation as well as beauty and majesty.

The structure of the tree carries many symbols. The circular base of the tree has no beginning or ending but a continuing connection. There are no sides or corners.

The branches are supportive of escape from those that mean harm. The leaves provide a comfort of shade from the harshness of the sun. The tree provides shelter from the elements.

In the story of Reb and Dran, there are gatherings at the baobab tree. It had become the main symbol of the forest. This tree stands approximately eighty feet tall. It is silhouetted against the sunset sky. It is a significant landmark near the countryside. It is convenient for the people to see as well as for the animals to dwell in.

It symbolizes strength, wisdom, and harmony for the entire forest. It symbolizes oneness and equality. It symbolizes the universe. It was fitting that the baobab tree is known for the resilience of individuals and communities in the face of changing circumstances.

It stands as the foundation in the forest where all animals can come together. It is neutral ground where all can feel a sense of importance and no threats.

The animals feel safety around the tree. They would make decisions without judgment but bring their wisdom and understanding.

It is an unspoken treaty zone. The peace treaty drawn is one of the big accomplishments at the tree. Each animal feels such a sense of accomplishment when they are leaving the tree.

The meeting for the animal protest as well as the meeting with Reb, the cougar, and the tiger are also done at the tree.

Reb has to escape several times when he is in danger, and the tree is the dependable source for his safety.

Dran does school reports on the mysteries of the baobab tree. He always finds the information fascinating, and he learns so much from his studies.

Dran and several of his friends challenge themselves to climb the baobab tree. It is an odd shape with smooth and shiny bark, which makes it even more difficult. When they attempt to climb, their clothes often turn pinkish gray or copper from the baobab tree's bark debris. After many attempts, they reach about one-third of the way up. That is twenty-five feet high.

The tree serves a great purpose for Dran as well. Because of the massive size of the base, it is ideal for many games they play. They love crawling on the trunk.

The tree is also known as the tree of life because of its remedies and traditions. The bark and the fruit are said to offer over three hundred sustaining uses. It is a plant that creates an entire habitat.

The leaves and the bark of the baobab treat diseases and provide nutrients.

The trees grow upside down, making their branches look like roots.

The fruit has a pale powder covering the seeds. It is rich in vitamins C and B2.

The leaves are an excellent source of protein.

The seeds are used as snacks and to thicken soups.

The symbolism of the tree carries comparisons to the tree of life.

The tree represents the connection between the earth and heaven.

The tree of life tells us that all living creatures are related.

The tree of life tells us that for billions of years, all life was microbial.

The tree of life is essential for things to evolve.

The tree of life reminds us that through extinction, some branches get cut down.

Many things about the baobab tree are parallel with the lives of Reb and Dran.

The tree thrives in a place where little can survive. The climate is not conducive to the growth of the baobab tree. But it strives anyway! It defies the odds.

The intertwining of Reb and Dran's lives also defies the odds.

The baobab tree adapts to its environment and continues to thrive.

Reb and Dran adjust to their environment and still thrive.

Baobabs are difficult to kill. If they are burnt or stripped, they will form new bark and keep growing. They are resilient.

In the lives of Reb and Dran, obstacles are faced, but they bounce back and renew their commitment to grow. They are resilient.

The mystery behind the baobab tree leads the bushmen to believe that it does not grow like other trees. They believe that they die from within. When they die, they suddenly crash to the ground with a thump and, one day, simply disappear.

In the life of Reb and Dran, when their clock strikes midnight, they simply slip away.

LIVE FAST before your clock strikes 12

Adventurous Reb

Throughout this book, you will see sketches of Reb, the bear that was done by Bryant LaShaun Ward. He was excited about being a part of this book project to honor his cousin who was an important part of his life. Not only were they merely 6 weeks difference in their age., they also shared an extremely strong comradery.

He sadly was not able to see this project to completion due to his passing.

I'm grateful for the role he played in the project with consistent encouragement and his art contributions. He was able to get it done before his clock struck 12.

Milton Keynes UK
Ingram Content Group UK Ltd.
UKHW050920121224
452350UK00020B/257